50 WANDA DRIVE

A Novella

GINGER MARIN

&

J BARTELL

DEDICATION

*This book is dedicated to our beloved feline family members
who gave us so much joy and companionship.*

CONTENTS

Chapter 1: Grommet 1

Chapter 2: Beef Jerky Bandits 13

Chapter 3: Bunkhouse Boogie................................ 31

Chapter 4: Ready or Not, Help's on the Way... Sort of..... 51

Chapter 5: Wine, Bread, and The Two Stooges 67

Chapter 6: Dirty Laundry and Bright-Eyed Raccoons....... 81

Chapter 7: Heads Will Roll................................... 93

Chapter 8: The Last Stand 109

Authors 123

CHAPTER ONE

GROMMET

The newspaper clipping was the first thing you'd notice. Pasted to a poster board and staked into the sun-baked dirt in front of an old western bunkhouse, it commanded attention with bold black headlines and smaller captions: "Hero housewife saves cat from certain death"; "Paige Martin & Friend." The faded newsprint showed two photos: a smiling woman with perfectly coiffed honey-blonde hair clutching a wide-eyed tabby cat, and a close-up of the cat's bewildered face.

Behind the poster, the bunkhouse squatted on a rustic California property, its weathered cedar siding bleached silver by decades of sun. Nestled in a shallow valley of wild grasses that turned golden each summer, the place sat just close enough to Napa to make weekend trips convenient, yet far enough that cell reception remained blissfully spotty. Uphill, connected by a winding gravel path lined with solar-powered garden lights, stood the main house—a sprawling structure where rough-hewn pine logs intersected with precisely cut river stone, all beneath a steep-pitched roof that shed winter rain and summer heat with equal efficiency.

A small party hummed beneath the cloudless California sky. The woman from the article, Paige Martin—forty-something with not a hair out of place, her manicured nails gleaming like polished shells—sat at the head of a wooden picnic table. Her clean-cut husband Eric, with salt-and-pepper temples and khaki shorts pressed to a knife's edge, hovered at her elbow. Wrapped and unwrapped presents of various sizes crowded the red-checkered tablecloth, a mountain of ribbons and tissue paper catching the afternoon breeze.

Their son Adam, who was 15 and wore classic Harry Potter-styled round eyeglasses, was hunched over reading a graphic novel at the end of the table. Next to him was Grandpa Billy who wore a washed-out blue shirt and a cap with the word *Veteran* on it; he was busy drawing a crude, almost childlike outline of a bomb in the dirt. With a smooth motion, he rubbed it away underfoot. Then he traced a cross. Another, and another, as his leg then his hand began to shake. Before anyone could notice, he obliterated them with the cane's tip, leaving nothing behind but disturbed dirt.

"Grommet's going to be kept busy," said Paige.

Eric slid over a wrapped gift. "Here, open this one."

Their friend Glen—a big man with a booming laugh who'd been working the cooler all afternoon—poked his wife Margie. "What's a Grommet?"

Margie pointed at the poster, her gold bangles jingling against each other. She was fifty, wore too much perfume, and had a neckline that plunged way too low. "The cat."

Glen could barely keep a straight face as Paige opened the gift and pulled out catnip spray.

"They said it was perfect for the lady who has everything," said Eric.

"Yep. Can't wait to try it on *you*."

Everyone laughed and Sue—plain, sensible linen trousers, the kind of woman who always brought the right side dish— slid over another one. "Open mine!"

Paige snatched and opened Sue's gift, ready for the next lame offering. Inside, a laser pointer. "Great, I have a choice of having a drugged out cat or a hyperactive one. Thanks, Sue."

Eric slid the pointer and the catnip over to a bunch of other opened toys as if they were beers across a bar counter.

Adam glanced up from his graphic novel long enough to examine the laser pointer with genuine interest, turning it over in his hands and clicking it twice to test the beam before setting it down. Then something caught his ear; he looked over at the group and shook his head at what he deemed to be utter stupidity—Sue's husband Reggie, a pudgy man with sweat stains blooming under his arms, announcing he had once tried catnip as a teenager to see if it was better than weed.

"Don't worry, they'll be gone soon," Grandpa said.

Glen got up noisily. "Who else wants a beer?" Sue's and Reggie's hands shot right up. Glen, already tipsy, moved to the bunkhouse while the others moved to the food table

About fifteen miles away, in a small high desert town, an old, beat-up car drove onto the quaint main street, passing a string of Mom and Pop stores. Each had a wooden sign out front and a bell on the door. It was like shifting into another decade, one at least fifty years old.

The car's dusty front bumper was duct-taped twice over while its back bumper had a hefty dent on one side. The car turned into an alley revealing a bold black and white sticker on the rear end: *God Hates You. That's Why!"*

Befitting the car, two low-lifes were inside. Reed, a 55-year-old deadbeat, was in the driver's seat, his face unshaven, and with an ugly neck scar peeking from under his shirt collar that was flipped up almost to his ears. He shoved a whiskey bottle under the front seat. Otis, his scrawny, half-wit brother, five years his senior, shoved a comic book under his own seat. There was a low hum of a country-western cassette tape, its volume barely registering as a presence. Reed pointed toward the windshield at the grocery store.

"Great. I'm starving," said Otis.

"Yeah, maybe you can get me some beef jerky instead of the steak I was looking forward to, you moron."

After the car stopped, Otis slunk around to the driver's side as Reed got out. "I said I was sorry," said Otis. "I didn't see the guard."

"Well, maybe if you were paying attention and not making funny faces at a kid." Reed's face morphed into a frustrated frown. "Shit, never mind."

"Now let's get us some gas money." Reed slipped on his black leather gloves, flexing his fingers to get the fit just right. His movements were slow and deliberate, a menacing foreboding of what was to come. Otis watched with a mix of awe and envy, his eyes widening in anticipation as he nervously awaited Reed's next words. "Where's the masks?" Reed asked.

Otis' heart skipped a beat. He checked the back seat then turned back around, embarrassed. "They're still in the other car." He cringed, waiting for the punch that never came.

Reed turned his head and spat a wad of disgusting phlegm but hadn't expected the gust of wind that blew the glop right through the open window onto the back seat. "That's on you, shithead!" stormed Reed.

Reed then led the way to the front entrance where they entered Wilson's grocery store. He observed a customer at the register with elderly Mrs. Wilson while Otis bee-lined to the beef jerky. He grabbed a bunch then looked over at Mr. Wilson who was stocking the freezer.

The ice machine rumbled loudly and the customer nodded to it. "Ice machine's on its last legs."

Mrs. Wilson chuckled, "I can't hear you over that darn ice machine!"

The customer laughed in kind, took his goods and left. Instantly, Reed whipped out his gun, causing Mrs. Wilson to jump and gasp. "Gimme the money, grandma." The old lady froze except for looking at her husband for support.

Otis zeroed in on Mr. Wilson, his supply of beef jerky in one hand, and a gun in the other. "Don't move, grandpa. I don't wanna hurt ya." Mr. Wilson raised his gloved hands— *black freezer gloves.*

Reed pounded the butt of his gun onto the ancient cash register. The drawer sprung open with a bang. He grabbed all the money, including the change. "Gimme the money in the safe."

Mr. Wilson yelled out, his voice wavering, "We don't have a safe."

"Everyone's got a fucking safe."

Otis hustled Mr. Wilson over to Reed, but distracted by the old man's gloves, dropped a bag of jerky. Mr. Wilson's foot, with each shuffling step, unknowingly nudged the bag across the floor. "You better tell him where it is," ordered Otis.

"He's telling the truth," whimpered Mrs. Wilson, "we take the money to the bank every day."

"Maybe they don't have a safe," said Otis.

"Shut up," countered Reed, who then punched poor Mr. Wilson in the face. The old man toppled to the floor as blood splattered. He lay crumpled and wheezing.

Reed kneeled and threatened to punch him again. The old man's teeth dropped out. Mrs. Wilson's throat seized up but she made a move toward her husband. Otis stopped her and, in the process, dropped another bag of jerky. "Come on Reed, you almost killed him. Let's go. We got the money."

Just then, a 6-year-old girl entered the store and the first thing she saw was the bloodied Mr. Wilson with Reed hunched over him. She froze. Reed stared at her. "Shit!" He then turned back to Mr. Wilson. "You shoulda had a safe." He stood and kicked the old man in the head.

Mrs. Wilson wailed helplessly as Reed then plowed over the girl and knocked her into a display case. Otis flinched hard, his gun hand dropping to his side. He took a half-step toward the girl, his mouth working like he wanted to say something, before the sound of Reed's boots on the linoleum snapped him back. He frantically tried to strip off Mr. Wilson's gloves but finally gave up, so he grabbed his dropped bags of jerky and ran out after Reed.

Back at the bunkhouse, Sue pointed to the potato salad and said to Paige, "Need more!"

"Yes, ma'am!" Paige grabbed the salad bowl and went to the bunkhouse to fill the order. As she neared the door, she heard Glen on the phone.

"You were right. She's actually taking this seriously. It's pathetic. Can't wait to get the hell…"

Paige spun around and dashed away. Sue's potato salad request would have to wait. She collapsed at the gift table and stared sullenly at the newspaper clipping on the poster—that ridiculous headline and her own frozen smile. Her throat tightened as she fiddled with a curled length of satin ribbon, twisting it between her fingers until it formed a tiny lasso. She flicked her wrist two times—each toss missing—before finally catching a fuzzy gray mouse cat toy and dragging it across the tablecloth.

Billy's white beard spilled over his collar like insulation. He noticed the storm cloud expression darkening her face and limped over, his cane leaving small divots in the soft ground. The wooden chair creaked in protest as he lowered his substantial frame beside her. "Okay, what's eating at you?" he asked, his voice gravelly from decades of cigarettes.

Her voice lowered to a whisper as she gestured at the party debris, the half-empty plastic cups. "I told them not to make such a spectacle of this, Dad."

"Hey, you deserve the attention." He patted her arm with a liver-spotted hand. "You put that abuser in his place."

"Actually," she sighed, "that abuser tripped and fell all on his own. I barely touched him."

"Well, he got what he deserved, anyway." Billy's beard quivered with conviction.

"Come on, Dad, he was Adam's age." She nodded toward her son, still hunched over his book. "Just a confused kid."

"Age has nothing to do with it," he said, thumping his cane once for emphasis.

"Why did it have to be me?" The mouse toy dangled limply from her fingers.

"Who the hell cares? Stop whining." His words cut through the afternoon air. "Life's not always fair. Sometimes you just gotta suck it up."

Paige's body tightened with frustration as she hurled the toy with a playful gesture, but her father's reflexes were still sharp as he caught it with ease. "See that? I still got it! Oh, by the way, I'm cooking up something special for the fourth. You're going to—"

"He didn't tell you, did he?"

"What?"

"I caught Adam trying to make those firecrackers we made last year and he almost blew a finger off. You told me you'd lock that stuff up."

"I thought I did. Well, I'll talk to him."

A gust of wind sent napkins and tissue paper scattering across the yard. Before anyone else reacted, Paige was already up—snatching the tablecloth corner with one hand, trapping the flyaway wrapping paper under her knee, and catching a rolling beer bottle with her foot before it hit the gravel. She had the table re-secured in seconds.

Eric watched, amused. "You missed your calling as a rodeo clown."

"With this crowd? I didn't miss it."

Back at the car, Otis haphazardly threw the jerky into the back seat. It landed right on the glop of spit. They both jumped in with Reed taking the wheel. He sped out of there, burning rubber.

Hearing the commotion, a middle-aged Deputy Hughes ran from the barbershop next door, face covered in thick shaving cream and gun in hand. At the same time, the injured girl ran out of the grocery store.

Mrs. Wilson then came out crying as she held onto the door frame. She pointed back inside. "George… he's…"

Deputy Hughes burst through the growing crowd and ran to her as she crumpled to the ground. "They killed George. Why?" she said.

The deputy peeked inside—gun drawn—where Mr. Wilson now stood holding a handgun left over from the great war. Startled by the deputy's presence, he fired. The bullet left a skid mark across Hughes' lathered-up face. Instinctively, Hughes unloaded his weapon, causing bullets to ping canned goods and the cash register. One ricocheted back at Hughes, skidding across the other side of his face. Mr. Wilson, mouth agape at the horror of it all, dropped dead of fright. The deputy, visibly shaken himself, backed away from the door.

A spectator stepped forward and tried to peek inside. Hughes quickly shut the door. "I think one of them fled out back. Need to secure the scene. Back off."

"You got it, deputy. But there was two of 'em in an old yellow Chevy. They headed north."

Suddenly, the driver of a muscle car roared up to the curb from who knows where. He must have been lost on his way to better parts or in need of some beef jerky. Hughes glanced over and saw the vehicle. He pulled the driver out. Hughes then slid behind the wheel, swerving away from the sidewalk and accelerating down the main street. He sent up a cloud of dust as he fishtailed and sped away.

"I'll call it in for ya," the spectator yelled after him. His voice cracked on the last word, competing with the muscle car's engine roar fading into the distance.

The muscle car driver's jaw hung slack, his eyes tracking the shrinking plume of dirt that marked where his ride had been seconds before.

Fifteen miles up the road, Paige gathered the last of the wrapping paper into a trash bag while the late afternoon shadows stretched long across the bunkhouse yard. Adam's wire-rimmed glasses slid down his nose as he picked at leftover potato salad. Grandpa sat at the far end of the table, his cane propped against his knee, his eyes half-closed.

Eric came up behind Paige and kissed the top of her head. He pulled the stuffed mouse toy from behind his back like a magician and dangled it in front of her. "For the record," he said, "I would've rescued that cat too. I just would've needed a ladder, a helmet, and probably an ambulance on standby."

Paige laughed—a real one, the first all afternoon. "You would've called a committee meeting first."

"Robert's Rules of Cat Rescue. Very important."

She swatted him with the mouse toy. For a moment, the afternoon felt like what it was supposed to be.

But somewhere down the road, a beat-up car tore through the afternoon, engine howling — a threat barreling closer with every mile.

CHAPTER TWO

BEEF JERKY BANDITS

After about five miles, Reed's speeding car stopped abruptly on a two-lane back road. They switched drivers, and when they took off again, Reed stripped off his black leather gloves and tossed them onto the dashboard, then, without looking, reached into the backseat and grabbed a bag of beef jerky.

As Otis flipped down the sun visor, a baggie of pills dropped into his lap. Without missing a beat, he tossed it to Reed. It landed right into the open package of beef jerky Reed was holding. Reed scowled, plucked the baggie out, and stuffed it into his shirt pocket — completely unaware that now both jerky spit and roadway dust were smeared on his crotch.

"She had more money, that dumb bitch. I know she was holding out."

"You were beating her fucking husband to death, Reed. She wouldn't hold out on you."

"What the hell do you know? Just drive the fucking car!"

"That's what I'm doing. I'm driving the fucking car."

Reed chomped down on a hard piece of jerky. "Jesus Christ." He looked closely at the bag. "Fucking expired." He spit the jerky out the window.

"Not like I had time to check the dates, you know." Otis looked into the rear-view mirror, then floored the gas pedal, jerking Reed's head back.

"Jesus Christ. What the fuck?! You gave me whiplash."

"We're being followed."

Reed glanced back and saw Deputy Hughes barreling down on them, gun blazing. He quickly clambered out the window and fired back, sending Hughes' car into a wild swerve. He fired off a second round, screaming at Otis to "blind 'em."

Otis veered onto the shoulder, catapulting a barrage of rocks and pebbles towards Hughes' windshield. The deputy was just able to activate his shoulder mic: "Debbie! Tell Murdock ... ten-twenty, Angeles Crest Highway, headed — " A rock burst through the windshield, sending a gust of air in and tearing any remaining foam from Hughes' face and hair and blinding him. The deputy's car careened off the road and tumbled down into a ravine.

Reed twisted in his seat to watch the deputy's car disappear into the ravine, his face contorting into a manic grin as he whooped with delight. "That's what you get, fuckface!" He punched Otis in the arm, making the car swerve slightly. "He almost caught us. Pull over; *I'll* drive."

They drove along the winding road, the sun beating down through the dusty windshield, casting shadows across the cracked vinyl dashboard. Reed fished the wrinkled pill baggy from his pocket, the plastic smudged with fingerprints and flecked with lint. He tipped two triangular, blue tablets into his palm, tossed them back, and chased them with amber whiskey from a half-empty bottle wedged between his thighs, his Adam's apple bobbling as he swallowed. Reed then extended both offerings toward his brother. Otis grabbed the whiskey bottle by its neck but waved away the pills, his eyes heavy-lidded with fatigue. "Stupid boring road," he muttered, taking a long pull that burned his throat. He wiped his mouth with the back of his hand, then slumped against the door, eyelids drooping as the monotonous hum of tires lulled him toward unconsciousness.

They sped past a car on the side of the road, hood propped open like a gaping mouth, steam still curling from its radiator. A half-mile further, they spotted a hitchhiker trudging along the sun-baked shoulder, sweat darkening the back of his faded denim shirt. He lugged a battered guitar case covered in band stickers and a small amp with frayed electrical tape holding the handle together. Reed jabbed Otis' ribs with his knuckles. "Hey... a music man... gonna be trouble in River City!" Reed cranked the wheel, tires crunching gravel as he pulled alongside the hitchhiker, a lanky guy with a three-day stubble and vintage aviator sunglasses with scratched lenses. "Not having much luck?" Reed asked.

The hitchhiker pushed his sunglasses up into his disheveled hair and squinted against the sun as he addressed Reed. "Got held up in town because of some shit going on. Now I'm two fucking hours late to a gig." He shifted his weight from foot to foot, gripping the guitar case handle so tightly his knuckles blanched. "Where you headed?" Reed's fingers drummed against the steering wheel.

"Fifty Wanda Drive. I think it's just a couple of miles from here up in the hills." The hitchhiker nodded toward the tree line.

Reed turned and muttered to Otis, a sharp grin spreading across his face, "I like it already."

"Maybe we should just keep going," Otis urged, his voice tight, like he was choking on the fear of getting caught if they wasted another second.

Reed shot Otis a fierce look, eyes narrowed to slits, then jerked his chin toward the door. Otis reluctantly reached back and popped the rear door lock. "Jump in," said Reed.

The hitchhiker hesitated, his eyes flicking nervously between the car and the distant road ahead. Driven by desperation, he slid in, guitar case clattering against the doorframe, bringing with him the smell of perspiration mixed with a generic drug store cologne. "Hey, thanks, man," he said.

As they drove off, Otis looked back at him. "You play guitar, huh? I always wanted to play but never got around to it." Reed laughed at the idea.

Instead of acknowledging Otis' fanciful desire, their guest simply said, "I'm Jimmy, by the way."

"Otis. He's Reed."

Reed spotted a small sign ahead, "Wanda Drive," and turned onto the dirt road. He looked every which way then started singing, "Help me Wanda, help, help me Wanda... so where the hell is Wanda? There's nothin' here."

"It's supposed to be at the end of the road," said Jimmy.

"Then why have a number? I mean if you're the only one on it."

Otis craned his neck like a nervous bird, scanning the dense pines that crowded the narrow road. His hands slapped against his thighs repeatedly, desperate to be the first to spot their destination. Then he spotted it — a weather-beaten, wooden sign with the number 50 carved deep and painted in flaking red. The rutted dirt road widened into a long gravel driveway that snaked between two massive oak trees. Reed gunned the engine and fishtailed into the makeshift parking area, kicking up dust that momentarily obscured a silver Lexus backing out, its tires crunching over scattered pine cones.

"Oh, shit, they're leaving," Jimmy said.

From the bunkhouse, Paige and Eric spotted the trio approaching. Reed lagged behind, chin lowered, as he thumbed a tablet from his breast pocket and discreetly popped it into his mouth while the others walked two paces ahead. Otis, fidgeting, kept yanking his collar straight, leaving smudgy fingerprints behind, while Jimmy walked easily, arms lugging his equipment, and eyes fixed on the bunkhouse porch.

"You found these guys, where?" Eric asked Paige.

"Craig's List."

"Damn, honey, you know how many people have been killed by using Craig's List?"

"Oh, stop, just because they're not wearing a suit and tie."

Overhearing the conversation, Grandpa interjected, "I told her to call the union. Union guys are never late."

"Shhh! They might hear you," Paige warned.

"I don't care if they do," Grandpa mumbled, as he limped off to his usual place at the table.

"Billy, you've turned into a grumpy old man and if you're not careful...," said Glen.

"What? I'll die a grumpy old man?"

Paige moved off to meet the entertainment, while Margie and Sue, both with their matching highlighted hair, zeroed in on Jimmy's faded jeans that hugged his thighs like shrink-wrap. "Here comes the entertainment," Margie said, nudging

Sue with a bony elbow, her gold bangles jingling. "And well-hung from the looks of it."

Sue popped Margie in the arm then burst out laughing, her lipstick slightly smudged at the corner of her mouth. "Margie! You're too much." Adam looked up from his paperback, squinting through his shaggy bangs, then exhaled a dramatic teenage sigh loudly enough to flutter the pages.

"Sorry I'm late," said Jimmy. "My car broke down. My buddies here gave me a ride."

"Oh, that's okay. I'm Paige. Eric's over there," she said as she led them to the bunkhouse. "You can set up near him."

Paige now noticed Adam reading his novel. "Adam, I asked you to help clean up." Adam sighed again, feeling put upon as usual. "Keep up that attitude and no computer for a week."

Adam rose and reluctantly moved to the bunkhouse. "It's all your friends. I don't see why I have to work."

"You could have had your friends over but they were too busy, remember?" Eric reminded him.

"Maybe if I lived near civilization."

"Civilization is a limitless multiplication of unnecessary necessities," Eric recited.

"Yeah, I know...Mark Twain. Maybe *he* liked living in the woods."

"That was Thoreau."

"Whatever."

Otis eyed the food as Reed checked out the women. "Nice spread," said Otis.

"Sure is," Reed agreed, still eyeing the women.

Margie and Sue now looked Reed and Otis over as Reed eyed the poster then moved closer to peruse the headlines. "Hero, huh?" he said under his breath, then snorted a laugh.

Margie, unimpressed with the men because of their unkempt appearance, wrinkled her nose disdainfully just as Paige came up with take-home food for them.

"So, Paige, you saved the best *and* the worst for last," whispered Margie.

"Oh, not you too!"

"Can you imagine what she'd be like if she'd been drinking?" said Sue.

Paige handed them the food bowls.

"Terrific! Glen will be eating this stuff for the next week."

"That's because you never feed him."

Margie burst out laughing.

"You sure you can't stay since they finally showed up?" asked Paige.

"Glen said his back's killing him."

Paige's smile tightened at the corners, Glen's earlier remark about her still stinging. "Think you can find your way back to civilization this time without a map?"

Margie's eyebrows knitted together as she glanced toward the winding dirt road.

"Eric! Our guests need an escort to the highway."

"I guess I have to," said Eric, "or they'll all be sleeping in the bunkhouse tonight."

"I'd rather be dead. I got standards you know." Margie chuckled.

Reed took note of the conversation. "Hey, no need to disturb your little party, I can lead them back. I got a great sense of direction."

"Oh, great. Thanks," said Paige. "Okay, Margie?"

Margie hesitated but Sue urged, "Come on. Let's go, already."

"I guess. Well, all right."

Margie and Sue gathered their food containers while their husbands stumbled toward their car.

"Oh, hey... mister..."

"Reed."

"When you get back," said Paige, "you can have a bite to eat before you continue on your way."

"Hell, yeah," said Otis, "that'd be great. I'm starved."

Jimmy positioned his fingers on the guitar strings when Reed nudged Otis. "You might as well stay here and get a head start."

Eric tossed a beer to Otis, who quickly popped it open. "I'm already starting," he laughed as he held up the bottle.

Reed settled behind the wheel of his rusted car, the door creaking like an old coffin lid as it closed. He gunned the engine twice, spewing white exhaust, then peeled out in front of Margie's Lexus, gravel pinging against both vehicles' undercarriages. As they disappeared down the winding dirt road, Jimmy's fingers danced across his guitar strings, producing piercing high notes that seemed to reverberate off the trees. Grandpa's leathery face contorted, his arthritic hands rising instinctively to cover his ears. Meanwhile, Otis hunched vulture-like over the buffet table, prying open every plastic container, shoveling spoonfuls of potato salad and cold cuts into his mouth, crumbs and grease dotting his chin.

"For the special lady," Jimmy said, as he nodded toward Paige then sang the blues.

"Not bad," Paige said to Grandpa.

"If I want the blues, I'll just look in the mirror."

Paige chortled as Grandpa headed to the main house at the top of the driveway.

Back at the table, Otis drained the last of his beer and reached into the cooler for another. He cracked it open, foam running down the side, and settled back with a contented grunt. Jimmy's music drifted through the late afternoon air. Otis tapped his foot, mouth full of potato salad, completely at ease — while somewhere down that dirt road, Reed was already at work.

Jimmy's music dwindled as Reed's rust-wagon lurched to a crooked halt on the narrow dirt shoulder of the road, its engine clattered to silence. Behind it, Margie's Lexus idled with a low, impatient growl. Reed emerged from his car. He reached through the open window, plucked his leather gloves off the dash, and pulled them on one at a time, flexing his fingers slowly until the fit was just right. The dappled sunlight caught the leather as he straightened up. His face was expressionless as he approached Margie's window, pleasantly enough, one hand raised in a casual wave — the gun in his right hand held behind his back until the last possible moment. When he raised it level with her temple, the barrel's blued steel looked almost black against her highlighted hair. "Everybody out! Slowly!" he commanded, his voice as dry as the dead pine needles underfoot.

Margie's throat produced a sound like a wounded animal as she stared cross-eyed at the weapon. In the passenger seat, Glen's alcohol-flushed face cracked into an oblivious grin, his words slurring as he waved a dismissive hand. "We just got in!"

"Out, asshole." Reed wrenched the door open and yanked Margie out by her arm, her gold bangles clanging against one another. Sue scrambled out while the husbands, reeking of alcohol, clawed uselessly at their door handles like trapped animals. "MOVE IT!" Reed's voice cracked like a whip. "I swear to Christ, I'll blow your fucking brains all over the road!"

Reed dug his fingers into Margie's spine, shoving her forward as the stench of fear filled the air. When they were all clear of the car, Reed rammed Glen with both hands, sending him staggering backward toward the tree line. "I protest..." Glen's face suddenly contorted. "Oh fuck, I'm gonna..." Vomit sprayed from his mouth in a violent arc.

Glen's and Reggie's eyes bulged at the gun now inches from their faces. Sue's breath came in shallow gasps as she clutched Reggie's arm, whispering with desperate, delusional hope, "Maybe he just wants the Lexus."

"Well, if he wants the damn thing," added Reggie, "then he's going to have to give us a ride home." Reggie then burped long and loudly.

"Well, that's disgusting and very inappropriate!" said Sue.

"Shut the fuck up, you two." Reed ripped a moneybag from his pocket and flicked it open --- blood still crusted on its zipper from the last poor bastard who'd owned it. "Wallets! Jewelry! NOW!" his voice tore into them. Reed then seized Margie by the back of her head, clutching her hair tightly in his fist, and pulled her face within inches of his. "You too, princess piggy!" Margie let out a sharp gasp, almost a choked cry as she struggled against his grip — her breath jagged, desperate, fear flooding her wide eyes. All of them scrambled to obey, trembling fingers fumbling with wallets, clasps and watches. Reed's patience snapped. He swung the bag, smacking them. "Can't you people just put your shit in a bag?" Sue clawed frantically at a rubber charity wristband. Reed's eyes flashed. "Are you fucking kidding? The GOOD stuff, bitch."

Glen's body convulsed as another stream of vomit erupted from him, splashing his shoes and the forest floor.

Reed shoved Margie back toward the others then noticed the wet patch creeping down Reggie's pant leg, the acrid smell of urine mixing with fear. A cruel smile twisted Reed's face. "Nobody fucking move," he said, "I got something special for you." He grabbed Margie's arm and dragged her toward his trunk. The metallic click of the latch was deafening. Margie expected to be hurled in along with the booty.

Sue's eyes darted wildly toward the tree line. "Run," she hissed through clenched teeth. Reggie's fingers dug into Sue's wrist as they bolted. Margie twisted in Reed's grip just in time to see Glen — her husband of twenty-five years — disappearing into the trees without a backward glance.

Reed's lips curled into a sneer as he watched the trio stumble toward the tree-line. "Oh, look at that, your hubby's making a break for it. You'd better go after him." He shoved Margie hard, sending her stumbling forward. She didn't hesitate; she ran like hell, her designer shoes kicking up dirt and snapping twigs. Reed watched her flee for three heartbeats, then tucked his weapon away before digging through his trunk. Inside, among a pile of clothing, water bottles, tools and junk, lay his prized possession — a machete with a worn wooden handle and a sharp blade with its edge notched from previous encounters. He wrapped his fingers around it, feeling the familiar weight. "Ready or not, here I come," he sang, voice lilting like a child's playground taunt.

He caught up to Margie in no time, her clumsy path through the underbrush making her easy prey, while the three up ahead stumbled through the woods, crashing through bushes like wounded animals. Further on, Reggie stumbled and fell. Sue pulled in vain to get him back on his feet as he grabbed her arm in a death grip. Meanwhile, Glen stood next to them, frozen.

"Help me," Sue pleaded.

Glen's bloodshot eyes darted frantically between the shadowy trees, his alcohol-soaked brain searching for escape. He pivoted on his heel, loafers slipping in the mulch as he lunged forward. Reed, with Margie in tow, had silently circled their position and extended one foot at the perfect moment. Glen crashed face-first into the forest floor, pine needles sticking into him and the taste of earth mixing in his mouth. Reed stepped hard on the back of Glen's neck. "You would leave your wife in the hands of someone like me, without even a fight?" He then stepped off. "Now, get up, you piece of shit."

Glen scrambled to his knees, spitting out soil and leaves. "Take my money — I've got plenty," he stammered, his hands frantically patting his empty pockets. His eyes widened with the sudden realization. Reed's laughter cut through the forest. "Please don't kill me," Glen whimpered, voice cracking.

"Me, me, me! What about your wife? Don't you want me to spare your wife?"

"Yes, please don't kill *us*."

"What about the other broad? You want me to set her free?"

Glen looked over at Sue. "Please, let her go."

Reed pulled Margie over to Sue. "Okay," he said, which caused Sue to let out a sigh of relief.

In a blink of an eye, he brought the machete down in a vicious arc, severing Reggie's hand at the wrist with a wet thunk that sounded like an axe splitting a watermelon. Blood sprayed in a crimson fan across Sue's blouse as Reggie's eyes bulged in disbelief. A guttural sound escaped his throat before yellowish vomit erupted from his mouth and he quickly lost consciousness. Glen scrambled backward, his shoes slipping on pine needles, before bolting between two trees, only to catch his foot on an exposed root. Sue remained frozen, her throat producing a high-pitched wail while Reggie's detached hand clung to her like a grotesque ornament, his middle finger caught in the tight elastic of her charity wristband, the fingers still twitching slightly as if trying to escape.

Reed muttered, "Here we go again," as Glen rose to his feet. In one swift motion, he pulled Margie down and snatched up a hefty rock, hurling it at Glen. It sent Glen crashing back to the ground. Yanking Margie back up, Reed trudged over to Glen and drove the machete into his back. "A pig in a poke," he sneered. "Or is that a poke in a puking pig?"

Margie wrenched herself free from Reed's grip and bolted into the woods. Reed cursed under his breath, then pivoted back to Sue, whose mascara-streaked face had gone chalk-white. He seized her trembling wrist, his fingers digging into the flesh where her pulse hammered wildly. "Come on. Let's go get your girlfriend." He dragged her stumbling through the underbrush, their feet churning up the musty rotten leaves' odor of the forest floor. "Call her. Go on."

Sue's throat constricted, her voice emerging as barely a whisper. "M... Margie."

Reed's veins bulged at his temples. "Call her like you mean it or I'll..." He waved the machete.

Sue's chest heaved as she summoned what little strength remained. "MAR-GIE!" The name tore from her lungs.

After a moment of tortured silence, Margie's frightened voice floated back at them. "Sue? Sue?" The words seemed to drift between the trees like lost spirits. "Where are you?"

Reed put the machete to Sue's throat and whispered, "Tell her."

"Over here. It's okay."

"And don't you fucking move," he instructed, as he rushed to conceal himself behind a tree.

"Where is he?" Margie forced out in a low, sharp voice.

"Not here."

Margie poked her head out from behind some trees and spotted that Sue was alone. She burst through the undergrowth toward her, then froze mid-stride at the sight of Reggie's severed hand still clutching her friend's wrist. A scream ripped from Margie's throat — raw, primal — as she pointed at Sue's arm. Sue's gaze dropped to the grotesque appendage, its knuckles white with posthumous grip. The realization that it remained attached sent her into hysterics — her howl splitting the air like an animal caught in a steel trap. Her body unable to move.

Reed lunged from his hiding place, his grip locked tight on the machete. He drove the blunt end of the handle into Margie's forehead. When it connected, it was with a hollow thud and her body crumpled like a marionette with cut strings, blood instantly soaking her blonde hair.

Reed's face contorted with savage pleasure as he now loomed over Sue, his machete correctly positioned for a deadlier strike. "You're the ugly one," he snarled, teeth gleaming, "and we all know what happens to you."

Sue raised her arm in self-defense, the one with Reggie's hand attached.

Reed's eyes flashed. "Don't you fucking raise your hands to me."

Reed's machete cleaved through Sue's arm just above the elbow with a wet, meaty thunk. Blood erupted in a crimson geyser, covering him from head to toe, as the severed limb spun away from her, Reggie's dead fingers still clutching her arm. Sue's scream died in her throat as her eyes rolled back, her body collapsing to the ground where she twitched once before going terrifyingly still. Reed then kicked the severed arm with the enthusiasm of a demented soccer player. The force of the kick separated the limbs mid-flight. They pirouetted through the air like some grotesque ballet — Sue's pale forearm and Reggie's disembodied hand reaching toward each other — a macabre parody of God and Adam reaching across the void in Michelangelo's Sistine Chapel masterpiece, before gravity reclaimed them and they flopped back to earth with a splat, now bizarrely holding hands.

Reed turned back to Margie who had gotten some life back into her.

Margie's eyes found his. Whatever noise she'd been making stopped. Her chin lifted slightly — a last, involuntary refusal to flinch.

"You're the pretty one and we all know what happens to you."

CHAPTER THREE

BUNKHOUSE BOOGIE

Back at the bunkhouse, Jimmy's fingers slowed on the guitar strings until the last bluesy note hung in the evening air like cigarette smoke. Otis, his face flushed from the alcohol, hoisted a half-empty beer bottle in salute, the liquid sloshing against the glass. A moment later, Reed's dusty car pulled in. Jimmy's calloused fingers instantly struck up another tune, something with a faster tempo.

Otis sauntered over to the car and popped his head in through the open window.

"Hey, you're wearing my clothes!" Otis said, noting Reed's change of clothing. Reed flashed a sly smile along with cash and credit cards. "You didn't hurt anyone, did ya?" Otis asked.

Reed stashed the money and cards into a secret compartment under the dashboard and exited the car. "Of course not. I don't always resort to violence when there's an easier way. I just do what I gotta do. Now I'm starved. Let's party."

"All right. But, let's not hurt anybody, okay? I mean, they're feeding us and all that. It wouldn't be right."

Reed clenched his teeth. "You're right, Otis. It just wouldn't be right." His smile didn't reach his eyes. "Now, how about you go to the house and see who's up there. Don't want any surprises." Reed slapped him on the back, a little too hard, as they neared the bunkhouse. Then he said to the group, "I took them all the way to the main road just to make sure."

"Great," said Paige.

"Hope there's something left," Reed said, indicating the table.

"Help yourself."

Paige felt something was different about Reed but couldn't put her finger on it.

"That's mighty friendly of you."

Otis reached into the cooler for a couple of beers and handed one to his brother as Reed sat at the table. Otis then said to Eric, "Hey, ah… I really could use a bathroom. Ya mind?" as he headed for the bunkhouse.

Paige pointed. "No… up at the house. That one doesn't work. Billy will let you in."

Otis glanced up to the main house and headed off with a wave and a smile. The house was rustic looking in stone and wood with a deep porch and a small but well-maintained garden. Parked in the driveway was a classic brown pickup truck with gleaming chrome accents next to a sleek black Lexus SUV and a hot red sports car. As he neared the car, he caught a whiff of newly waxed metal, leathery upholstery and piney air fresheners. "Snazzy," he said.

At the front door, Otis swiveled his head like a prison searchlight, scanning for witnesses. No extra kids or yapping dogs were lurking. A dwarf kumquat tree caught his attention, its branches heavy with bright orange-yellow fruit that looked like tiny globes against the dark green leaves. He plucked three, feeling their firm, waxy skin between his fingers before popping one into his mouth. The burst of tangy sweetness made him wince and smile at the same time. He raised his knuckles to knock, hesitated, then tried the brass doorknob instead. It turned with a smooth click — unlocked. Otis slipped inside, easing the heavy oak door shut behind him with barely a whisper. He crushed another kumquat between his teeth, the juice trickling down his throat, as he pocketed the other one. Otis then tilted his head and listened to the muffled sounds of the house — a clock ticking somewhere, the hum of a refrigerator, the faint melody of music — before padding across the polished hardwood floor of the living room.

Otis ran his fingers along the music center, TV console, framed pictures, books, and other objects, admiring all the things he would never have. He stepped through into the office area where he saw a desk, computer, pictures of Eric in a suit with others in front of a bank, shaking hands at a ribbon-cutting ceremony. Otis threw his shoulders back, acted like he was straightening his tie, and mimed shaking hands with an imaginary line of important people. There were a few photos of Paige, posing with Adam, in Western gear and riding a horse, lassoing a fake cow, lassoing Eric. Otis grinned and twirled a pretend lasso. With each thing he encountered, he grew envious, yet a little mellow at the same time. He imagined himself as the lucky stiff with a beautiful home and a beautiful family.

Gentle music came from a back room. Otis followed the sound to Grandpa Billy's room where the door was left slightly ajar. He peeked in and saw Billy napping, his mouth slightly open, one hand resting on his chest, then closed the door and continued to case the house.

In the guest bathroom, Otis took a piss and hummed to the soft music. He accidentally let out a fart so he grabbed the can of freshener from the back of the toilet tank. One long spray. He breathed in the scent. Almost the same citrus scent as the kumquat he had just eaten. He tried to pop the last one into his mouth but missed. It bounced off the floor and landed in a cat litter box, right next to a piece of half-covered over shit. He stared, trying to decide if he should pick it out. Finally, he reached down and gently picked up the kumquat, wiped it on his pants and studied it carefully. Maybe it was still good, he thought. It hadn't actually landed on the shit. Nah. He tossed it back in the box where this time it really did land on the shit.

A pair of yellow eyes glinted from beneath the fancy, claw-footed tub. Grommet, the cat, had watched the entire bathroom episode. Once the stranger's footsteps faded, he emerged, padded to the litter box, and with precise calculation, batted the kumquat across the tile floor with a forceful paw — sending it sailing like a golf ball rescued from a sand trap.

As Otis headed back down the driveway toward the bunkhouse, Paige was coming up the drive. "You find it okay?"

"No problem."

After they passed each other, Otis twirled around and watched as Paige went to the house. He chuckled and continued on his own way, then said under his breath, "Sorry, lady. You been real nice… but business is business." He spotted a small bird sitting on a tree limb. "Hey there little birdie. The party's this way. Follow me and I'll give ya some crumbs." The bird elicited a loud chirp and flew off in the other direction. "Stupid bird."

Paige entered Billy's room after knocking lightly. "Dad…"

Billy stirred. "Huh?"

The music had already cut out on the radio, leaving only the fading snippet of a news report about a crime in the small town a few miles away. Paige caught only a few words before it drifted into a another song. She pushed it out of her mind.

"Dad, come back down and say goodbye to the fellas, okay? It's getting late."

Back at the bunkhouse, Paige and Eric gathered empty plates and beer bottles while Jimmy's music drifted through the early evening air, courtesy of the CD he brought. Jimmy had finally settled in with a plate of food, Adam watching him eat from the next chair over. Billy sat at the far end of the table, happily munching on a protein bar and hoping the event would finally come to an end so he could say his goodbyes and good riddance.

Paige moved around the table, stacking plates. Her eyes went to Reed, sitting at the far end. He was eating and smiling and saying nothing. Whatever it was she'd noticed when he drove back in was still there, nagging at the back of her skull.

Reed and Otis sat at the other end, still chowing down. "These guys got a load of money, a fucking bank full," Otis whispered.

"Yeah, what do you know?" Reed asked skeptically.

"I know what I know."

Reed saw Eric was busy in the bunkhouse, so he looked over to Adam. "Hey, kid, what does your father do?"

"Bank manager. Why?"

"Looks like one, that's all." Reed's face lit up. He turned back to Otis, giving him a quick, conspiratorial wink that lasted just long enough for a silent understanding to pass between them.

Adam, oblivious to the exchange, turned his attention back to Jimmy while fidgeting with a plastic water bottle cap in his hands. "So, do you, like, know any rock music or what?"

"Sure. But I thought for this group, blues was a safe bet."

"What about Country-Western?" Reed asked.

Eric exited the bunkhouse just in time to hear that. "Country-Western? All that crying and whining, who can stand it?" He laughed.

Reed winced, just slightly, like the comment had landed somewhere personal.

"Hey, I like the blues," said Otis. "If I played the guitar, I'd play the blues."

"You *are* the blues," said Reed.

"What the hell does that mean?"

"So, how about Country-Western?" Reed asked Jimmy again.

"Why aren't you in the union?" Grandpa Billy suddenly demanded of Jimmy.

Reed seethed silently as he was interrupted and ignored yet again, his jaw tightening as if he were swallowing something bitter.

"As you might have guessed," said Eric, "Billy used to be in the union."

"Yeah? What instrument did you play?" Jimmy asked.

"Violin."

"With those fingers?" Jimmy and Adam laughed as they eyed Billy's fat fingers.

Reed pretended to be amused and chuckled along for a second or two before saying, "Bet you could shoot off a .44-mag out here and no one would even hear it."

"We hear hunters shooting all the time," said Grandpa. "Hardly pay attention anymore."

Otis caught the subtle movement — Reed's fingers disappearing one by one into those black leather gloves, creaking softly as he flexed his fingers.

"Okay, Gentlemen," said Eric, his voice carrying the practiced authority of someone used to ending business meetings, "thanks for bringing our musician. But the party is now officially over. Jimmy, I'll call triple A for —"

The sound of Reed's fist hitting the wooden table echoed like a gunshot, rattling a few serving dishes and whatever else was left on the table. His face twisted into something feral as he leaned forward. "I think Jimmy boy should play another fucking tune. And, it'd better be Country-Western."

The air seemed to crystallize around them. Adam's water bottle froze halfway to his mouth; Paige's smile evaporated;

Grandpa Billy's rheumy eyes widened with recognition of the danger.

"I'm not through having fun yet," Reed sneered.

Eric's jaw clamped as he squared his shoulders. "Yes, I think you are," he said, his banker's voice hardening with an authority that rarely needed to be tested.

Reed's face hardened. In one fluid motion, he snatched his half-empty beer bottle and hurled it with a vicious sidearm throw. The amber glass smashed against Eric's temple with a sickening crack. Dark beer and blood sprayed out as Eric crumpled, his knees buckling beneath him.

"ERIC!" Paige screamed, her face draining of all color.

Reed kicked his chair backward, the wooden legs scraping harshly against the dirt. His hand disappeared beneath his jacket and emerged gripping his pistol, the barrel sweeping across the frozen faces around the table. Even Otis' mouth hung open in shock until Reed's cold stare bored into him. Otis fumbled for his own gun; it caught on his jacket pocket before he yanked it free.

"Now we're really gonna have a party," declared Reed.

Paige bolted to Eric who was bloodied and rising slowly. "I... I'm okay," he sputtered. But Otis blocked her. Paige's eyes shifted between Eric, Reed and Otis. Eric then moved back to the table and tried to sit.

"No, you don't, yuppie man," Reed shouted.

"Please, let him sit down," begged Paige.

"Simon didn't say 'sit'. And Simon sure as fuck didn't say stand, either." Reed slammed the butt of his gun against the side of Eric's head, knocking him unconscious.

Paige gasped and clenched her fists helplessly. Grandpa limped up behind Reed, cane in hand, ready to strike.

"Hey, Reed, turn around," Otis said with a chuckle.

Reed turned and laughed as he watched Grandpa make his approach.

"Dad, don't!" Paige screamed, as Adam ran toward his father.

"Otis, take that old coot and tie him down somewhere."

Otis grabbed Grandpa's cane and shoved him toward the bunkhouse. "Come on, old man."

With a savage yank, Reed tore Adam away from his father's body, then gestured with his gun for both the boy and Paige to step back. Meanwhile, Jimmy, holding his amp and guitar, slunk toward the woods. Reed turned and spotted him through the trees. "Now will you look at that... our entertainment's leaving."

Just then, Otis pushed Grandpa out of the bunkhouse — bound and fuming in an old wheelchair he'd dug up from inside. "Hey, Reed, look what I found." The chair's wheels squeaked against the dirt as Grandpa struggled against the ropes, trying to topple the whole contraption.

Reed motioned for Otis to give chase just as Jimmy swiveled and locked eyes with Reed — and ran. "Come on, Reed. He's a good guy. He won't squeal."

Reed shot Otis an evil look, then indicating the Martins, said, "Watch 'em." He chased after Jimmy himself.

Dismayed, Otis turned his focus on the family. "Shit, he had to go and leave. See that? That's what happens when you piss Reed off. You're nice people. Now go sit down."

Paige and Adam glanced from Eric in the dirt to Grandpa struggling on the porch in the wheelchair. Otis gestured for them to come to the table with a wave of his gun. Suddenly, a loud bang echoed from the woods. Everyone's eyes quickly shifted in that direction.

Jimmy was on his knees, his upper thigh bloodied. He dropped his guitar and amp and tried to crawl away, but Reed ran up, jumped on his back, and rode him like a pony, laughing and kicking Jimmy in the sides. He hopped off and pulled Jimmy around to face him then shoved his gun up under his chin and waited.

Jimmy tried to sing the opening lyrics to Garth Brooks' "Friends in Low Places," tears streaming, choking on the words.

After a few lines, an amused Reed said, "I guess that yuppie man was right. All the crying and whining, who can stand it?" He pulled the trigger.

Reed reappeared at the bunkhouse carrying Jimmy's guitar. With a reckless swing, he hurled it toward Otis — not aiming to hit, but to make a point. "Here's that fucking guitar you always wanted." The guitar slammed against the bunkhouse wall, echoing the tension between them. Reed moved up close to Otis. "Next time you do what I tell ya or I'll blow *your* fucking head off." Shaken, Otis retreated, his hands trembling as Reed's eyes now bored into the huddled family.

"Sons-of-bitches… loser-punks!" Grandpa roared, his voice cracking into a rough rasp. He coughed hard, catching his breath. "That's what you are. No excuse for you."

"Hey, Gramps, no name calling," Otis said. "I don't like no name-calling."

"Otis, get that old fuck outta my sight!"

"What about Jimmy?"

"What about him?"

"You want maybe I should bury him or something?"

"No. I want maybe the bears should eat him."

Otis looked around nervously for bears. "There's bears here?"

"How the fuck would I know?" Reed turned to the Martins. "You got bears?"

Paige and Adam stared at him, refusing to spill the beans.

"Fuck the bears. Move it."

Otis pushed Grandpa back into the bunkhouse. The old man struggled and cursed, trying to topple his wheelchair. "If I had two good legs, I'd stomp you into the ground. Cowards."

Reed reloaded his weapon, keeping an eye on his hostages. "Shut up, you fat-fingered fuck."

After Otis came back out of the bunkhouse, Reed saw him pick up and examine the now broken guitar. "Shit, okay. Go bury him. Make it fast."

Otis ran back into the bunkhouse as Reed moved toward Paige and Adam. "The jewelry. You too, kid, gimme the watch."

Otis zipped by carrying a shovel and dark gardening gloves.

Adam held out his watch and Reed pocketed it, then pointed to Eric. "Him too."

"I'll do it," said Paige.

"No, I want the kid to do it."

Paige nodded grimly at her son. Adam shuffled to his father's side and dropped to one knee. His fingers trembled against his father's wrist as he unclasped the watch, then dug into Eric's pocket for his wallet. "Sorry, dad," he whispered, whimpering. He rose with both items clutched in his fist, and placed them in Reed's outstretched palm.

"Good boy, now go sit down."

Paige fumbled with the clasp of her necklace, but before she could manage it, Reed strode over, seized her arm, and dragged her over to a chair. As they were passing the gift table, she spotted the laser pointer cat toy. She ran her hand along the table and snatched it.

Reed took a seat and pulled her onto his lap sideways. "Let me help ya." He fingered her hair, neck and necklace.

"Leave my mom alone."

Reed looked at Adam. "Shut it, kid, you might learn something."

As the twilight deepened, a single light on the top of the bunkhouse flickered on, casting long shadows over the desperate gathering.

Paige seized her chance — raising the laser pointer and flashing it straight into Reed's eyes, buying herself precious seconds.

"Fuck!"

She pushed off Reed's chair forcefully, sending him crashing to the ground with a hard thud. His gun slid away from him, coming to rest at her feet. In a frenzied motion, Paige dropped the laser pointer and lunged for the gun. She raised it, hands trembling in fear and rage, and said, "Don't think for one second I don't know how to use this."

Reed blinked rapidly, his vision still distorted. "You holding my own piece on me?" A manic cackle erupted from his throat as he squinted up at her.

Paige called out to Adam. "Get Grandpa." Adam bolted to the bunkhouse, flung open the door and released Grandpa from his wheelchair trap. They came back out, prompting Paige to yell back at Adam, "Get the rope."

"What rope?" Adam screamed.

She pointed to the coiled up rope on a hook on the porch and said, "Dad, come here."

Adam brought the rope. Paige took it with both hands, and as she did she held the gun out to Grandpa — she was going to need both hands to work the lasso. "Stay down!" she told Reed. Grandpa took the gun and aimed it at Reed without a word.

With the rope in hand, Paige fumbled but managed to make a lasso and maneuver herself cautiously toward Reed. He had recovered enough to see what was going on. "That old coot won't shoot me. He's too fucking scared."

"I got a bunch of battles and two wars under my belt, bucko. You aiming to make it three?"

Reed tried to get to his feet while keeping his eye on Grandpa. With his eyes off Paige for that moment, she looped the rope around his neck and pulled it tight. Still on the ground, Reed grabbed at the rope to keep from choking. Furious, he kicked the furniture and threw dirt with his free hand.

Grandpa shouted, "Stop moving!"

Paige tied the other end around the bunkhouse post. "Dad, knife."

Grandpa dug into his pocket and pulled out a pocketknife that he tossed her way. It fell short so she rushed to grab it before the tables got turned on her. Paige then was able to cut a length of rope and made another lasso. After a second try, she looped it around Reed's foot. He kicked out violently.

Grandpa moved closer to Reed. "I'll shoot your dick off."

Reed spat at Grandpa. It missed.

"Your spit isn't worth spit."

Reed spat again. It still missed.

"This is how you spit." Grandpa hawked a wallop and spat it out, landing on Reed's crotch.

Paige yanked on the rope and tied it to a tree. Reed was stretched thin.

"Take care of Eric," Grandpa said. "And keep an eye out for the other guy."

Paige rushed to Eric who was now beginning to regain consciousness. She told Adam, "Call nine-one-one."

Adam, his heart pounding into his ears, ran to the bunkhouse just as a shot, coming from the direction Otis went, landed at Grandpa's feet. The sound was like a cannon blast and made Adam skid to a halt. The tiniest bit of dirt sprayed up into the air, barely missing Adam's arm as he dove for cover. Grandpa leaped up to avoid the bullet and whirled. He lost balance and fell backward, dropping the gun. Paige spun around and dove for it. She landed just short of it and, as she hit the ground, bullets flew around, spitting dirt on her. She lost the pocket knife too when it skidded away from her. Adam crawled over to shield his father with his body.

Otis came up alongside Paige and picked up Reed's gun. Now back on his feet, Grandpa, still a bit dazed, retrieved the pocket knife.

"Get me the fuck out of this," screamed Reed.

Otis turned to see Grandpa bearing down on Reed. But just before Otis fired off another round, Grandpa grabbed his head in pain and collapsed on top of Reed.

"Grandpa!"

"Dad!"

Reed struggled against the hefty weight of Grandpa Billy.

"Why, old man? Why?" said Otis, "Goddammit. Look what you made me do."

As Paige ran to Eric and Adam, Reed screamed, "Get this fat fuck off me."

Otis pulled Grandpa, who was unconscious, off and untied Reed who got back on his feet. "Motherfuckers," he shouted, spit flying out of his mouth. He then rushed over, and, lightning fast, grabbed Paige by the neck. His fingers, caked with grime and blood, dug into her neck like steel claws. She tore at him, scratching his chest and neck. His grip tightened on her throat as he raised her higher. Her toes barely touched the ground. She felt a searing pain in her neck, but she did not stop struggling.

Reed hauled Paige across the dirt toward Grandpa's motionless body. "That's on you, bitch," he snarled, then flung her down. The impact knocked the wind out of her. As she gasped for air, her fingers brushed something cold by Grandpa's hip — his pocketknife. Her hand closed around it, and she pushed herself upright, legs trembling but stance wide, the blade extended toward Reed. He stared at her, his lips curling into a sneer. "Well, look at you. You're a fighter, I'll give you that." When Otis moved forward, Reed's hand shot out, stopping him. His eyes never left Paige as he beckoned with his fingers. "Let's see what you got, mama."

Adam cried, "Mom… don't." Paige looked over at him then back to Reed, steely-eyed, ready to fight.

Reed smiled and took the rope he was tied with and whipped her with it. "You like ropes." The rope whipped through the air with a loud crack and Paige cried out in pain. She grabbed the end of it but Reed pulled hard and yanked her to the ground and loomed over her like a predator looking to devour his capture. Paige's grunts of determination were punctuated by her teeth gritting against each other as she tried to get the better of him. She quickly got to her feet again, wielding the knife, as Reed was still snapping the rope at her.

She tried to stab him. "You give me anymore shit, bitch, and I'll ride you wet and hard," he said.

"It's ride 'em hard and put 'em away wet… you asshole," spewed Paige.

Reed charged forward, clamping his fingers around her wrist, twisting it until the knife point hovered just inches from her jugular. Paige strained backward, muscles trembling, as the blade inched closer. From the corner of her eye, she saw a blur of movement — Adam hurling himself forward, the canister of catnip spray clutched in his hand, its contents hissing into Reed's face.

"Mother…fucker!" Reed's curse tore through the air as he lashed out blindly, the knife-hand connecting with Adam's jaw in a sickening crack while his elbow drove into Paige's solar plexus. She crumpled. Adam lay sprawled where he fell, limbs leaden, while Reed clawed at his burning eyes, spitting and cursing through ragged breaths.

Otis rocked his head in his hands. "God almighty, you're killing 'em all, Reed. You promised you wouldn't."

With his vision mostly cleared, Reed grabbed his brother by the collar. "They're killing "

me, you imbecile. And what have you been doing? Sitting like a dog scratching your waxy ears."

"Let's just get outta here," Otis cried.

"And leave a bank full of money? And they ain't all dead. So shut the fuck up and help."

"What…what am I supposed to do?"

"Get rid of the old fart. And I'll take the yuppies to the house. This thing ain't over until I say it is."

Reed stalked over to Eric. He seized Eric's face between his calloused fingers, squeezing until the skin blanched white around his grip, and delivered a stinging slap that echoed like a branch snapping. Yanking Eric's head to the side, he forced him to look where Adam and Paige lay sprawled in the dirt, their limbs twisted at unnatural angles, chests barely rising with shallow breaths. "See? The happy little family ain't no more." A cruel smile split Reed's face as he released his grip, letting Eric's head thump against the ground. "God, I hate families," he spat, a thread of saliva dangling from his lower lip.

"Hey, I'm your family," said Otis. "You don't hate me, do you?"

Reed's eyes bored into Otis, daring him to say another word.

On the ground, Paige lay still. She didn't let on that she was conscious. Above her, Reed's boots shifted in the dirt. His voice, when it came, was flat and certain — the voice of a man who had already decided what happened next. She pressed her palm flat against the cold earth and made herself breathe slow. It wasn't over. Not even close.

CHAPTER FOUR

READY OR NOT, HELP'S ON THE WAY… SORT OF

By the time Reed marched them up the gravel path and through the front door, Paige couldn't feel her hands. She and Adam had hauled Eric between them the whole way, his feet dragging furrows in the dirt. Reed shoved them into the corner of the living room floor, Eric down first, then disappeared down the hall toward the office. A moment later they heard him on the phone.

Reed paced the office, phone pressed against his ear. Four rings later, a gravelly male voice answered. "Yeah?"

"I got a job for ya," Reed said. On the other end was Garvey, a mountain of tattooed flesh with a nipple ring, sprawled across rumpled sheets in a bedroom that reeked of stale cigarettes and cheap cologne. His girlfriend Cindy, fifty going on thirty, draped herself across his barrel chest. Her bleach-blonde hair was cropped close on one side, revealing a large, dangling earring shaped like a question mark with a sparkling cubic zirconia at the tip. Her other ear wore a constellation of silver piercings while faded snake tattoos slithered up her arms.

"What's up?" Garvey asked.

Cindy's crimson-painted lips brushed his ear. "I hope you are." Her fingers, adorned with chipped black polish, traced circles around his nipple ring before reaching down between his legs.

"A nice bank job." Reed replied, voice dropping to a conspiratorial whisper.

Garvey instantly swatted her hand away. "Yeah? What's the deal?"

"I'll tell ya when ya get here."

"Tell me now." Moonlight filtered through torn blinds, casting prison-bar shadows across the bed. Cindy's teeth grazed Garvey's earlobe, her breath hot against his skin as she strained to hear the conversation.

"Stop fucking around," Reed snapped.

Cindy's eyes widened. "How'd he know?" she whispered, pulling back slightly.

"Grab a fucking pencil and get here fast."

Garvey grabbed a pen from the side table and scrawled the address Reed gave him onto Cindy's thigh. "Got it."

Reed slammed the phone down.

Garvey's fingers punched in a number on his phone, the bedsprings creaking as he shifted his weight.

In a darkened apartment, Travis' thunderous snoring wrestled with the flickering TV until a shrill ring cut through both. A hairy arm dragged itself from the tangled sheets, fingers fumbling for the nightstand light, sending a parade of cockroaches darting along the baseboards. He snatched the phone. "Talk," he mumbled, his voice heavy with sleep and the dull haze of whiskey downed earlier in the day.

Garvey's words crackled through the line. "I got a job for ya."

"What's up?" Travis scratched his stubbled chin, eyes closed.

"A fucking bank job."

"What's the deal?" Travis's free hand disappeared beneath the sheets, moving rhythmically.

"I'll tell ya when ya get here."

"Tell me now." The movement quickened.

"Stop fucking around."

Travis froze mid-stroke, blinking in confusion.

"Just get here fast."

Across town in a cramped bathroom with peeling linoleum, Bonnet perched on a toilet seat, his weathered face illuminated by the glossy pages of a dog-eared Playboy. The phone's buzz made him curse as he juggled the magazine, trying to extract the device from his sagging jeans without losing his place. "What?" he barked, one eye still fixed on Miss September.

Garvey again. "I got a job for ya."

"What's up?" A drop of sweat trickled down Bonnet's temple.

"A fucking bank job."

"Okay, what's the deal?" Bonnet fumbled with the speaker button, the phone clattering to the grimy floor as he tore off a wad of toilet paper, gaze never leaving the centerfold's airbrushed curves.

"I'll tell ya when ya get here."

"Tell me now."

"Stop fucking around."

The toilet flushed with a gurgling roar as Bonnet stood, magazine still clutched in his nicotine-stained fingers.

"Just get here fast."

Paige and Adam struggled to keep their sobs silent, their faces streaked with tears as they half-carried, half-dragged Eric's bloodied body to the leather sectional. Eric's head lolled forward, a thin crimson line trickling from his temple down to his jawline.

When Reed returned to the living room, he saw Otis and snatched the half-empty bottle of Jack Daniel's from his grimy fingers, taking a long swig while gesturing with his pistol toward the Martins. "Put him back in that corner. Now!" They reluctantly followed Reed's orders, shuffling back across the floor, then carefully lowering Eric down. Reed wiped his mouth with the back of his hand and nodded to Otis, whose face glistened with sweat. "Now really go through this place. Every drawer, every closet."

Otis disappeared into the hallway, his footsteps heavy against the hardwood. Reed swiveled toward Paige and Adam, jabbing his gun toward the sofa. "You two, sit down."

"There's a safe in the bedroom," Otis called out a moment later.

Reed's eyes lit up. "Get back here," he yelled. When Otis re-entered the room, his eyes darted between Reed and the hostages. "Watch 'em," Reed ordered.

Reed grabbed Paige by the arm and pushed her down the hallway where Otis had pointed. In Grandpa Billy's bedroom, they faced a gun safe tucked into the corner of the walk-in closet. Reed jabbed his gun against her spine. "Open it."

Paige hesitated, prompting Reed to call out, "Otis, ya got your gun on the kid?"

Otis waved his gun haphazardly toward Eric and Adam while he grabbed jelly beans from a bowl on the coffee table. "Right between the eyes."

"Count to ten, then blow his head off."

Paige hurriedly opened the safe.

"Don't shoot the kid."

"Okie-dokey" said Otis, as he popped the last jelly bean in his mouth.

Reed pushed Paige away from the safe and drooled over the contents — a shotgun and handguns. "She's coming out." He motioned for her to leave.

"I hear ya!"

Paige came back into the living room and Otis trained his gun now in her direction, motioning for her to join Eric and Adam, who was now sitting on the floor next to his father. Paige lowered herself to the floor between them. Her eyes swept the room, then the hallway, then back again. No sign of her father. Just the dark at the end of the hall and whatever was out there beyond the front door.

"Where's my father?"

Otis kept his eyes on his gun.

"Otis." Her voice dropped. "What did you do with him?"

"He's…" Otis scratched the back of his neck. "He's taken care of."

"Taken care of." She stared at him. "What does that mean?"

"It means what it means." He shifted his weight and looked at the wall.

"Is he alive?"

Otis said nothing, which was its own kind of answer, except it wasn't — not really — because he couldn't quite bring himself to say the word either way. He just scratched his neck again and looked somewhere that wasn't her face.

Paige turned away, her spine stiffening, a dangerous glint hardening in her gaze as she pulled Adam close.

About an hour or so later, Otis was enjoying a high-speed chase on the local TV news and eating potato chips, as Paige and Adam were still on the floor, but now with wrists tied behind them and their ankles cinched, while Eric slept.

Paige spotted a cat toy under a chair. She whispered to Adam, "Where's the cat?"

"What?"

"Grommet. Where's Grommet?" Adam glanced around, then shrugged. Paige kept her eyes peeled.

Bored with the TV and now out of potato chips, Otis licked the salt off his fingers, then wiped left-over grease on his stained jeans before lumbering down the hallway to join Reed in the master bedroom. He found Reed wearing one of Eric's pale blue button-down shirts, the fabric straining slightly across his broader shoulders as he rummaged through the cedar-scented walk-in closet. Otis grabbed a crisp tan Oxford shirt and threw on a navy Brooks Brothers sport coat over it, the sleeves dangling past his knuckles. They stood side by side, admiring themselves in the full-length mirror mounted on the closet door. In Otis' case, the clothes hung from his bony frame like expensive drapes on a wire hanger, the shoulders drooping and the collar gaping around his scrawny neck, making him look like a well-dressed scarecrow who'd lost half his stuffing.

Reed took a close look at his own face. "Could use a shave… just the thing to set off the duds, whaddya think?"

"You look good. I haven't seen you in such good clothes since… well, since never."

"Fucking yuppie shit… thought he'd have some of those shirts with the alligator…hey, you know, I don't look too bad in yuppie clothes."

"Yeah, you look good. What about me, don't I look good?"

Reed perused the room then opened the bathroom door. Hiding under the bed, eyeing their feet, was the cat. "Better get out there and watch 'em." Reed then entered the bathroom.

"Come on, Reed, I gave you a compliment. You could gimme one."

Reed stepped out of the bathroom with a stern look on his face causing Otis to back up nervously. He stretched out his hands and straightened Otis' shirt collar. "You're my brother. Of course you look great. You nail the back door shut, like I told ya?"

Otis beamed from Reed's compliment. "I always do like you tell me."

Reed patted Otis' face in recognition — a little too hard. He then sauntered back to the bathroom where he rifled through the medicine cabinet. Front and center was Xanax, a nearly full bottle. He popped a few, swilling them down with a slug of whiskey, relishing the taste of both.

When Reed returned to the living room, he went over to Eric who was weak but now conscious. Blood had dried in a rust-colored trail down the side of Eric's face, his eyelids fluttering as he struggled to focus. Reed squatted to face him, his knees popping, and pulled out Grandpa's pocket knife. His breath reeked of whiskey as he leaned in close enough for Eric to see the yellow stains on his teeth. "Here's the deal. I'm gonna ask you some questions. And if you lie, I start cutting into that stupid-looking kid of yours, ya got it?"

Eric nodded weakly.

"How much money in the bank?"

"A million and a half."

Reed's eyes widened, shocked. "What did you say?"

"Holy shit!" said Otis, who was standing nearby.

Reed grabbed Eric's shirt and pulled him in close. "Don't you bullshit me."

"The money's for the farm workers."

Reed studied Eric's face, searching for any hint of deception. "Okay. How do I get it?" Eric blinked, his eyes shifting away as he tried to think of a response. He opened his mouth and then closed it, his lips pressed together in a thin line.

Reed straightened up, turned away from Eric, and stared at the wall for a moment. When he looked back at Otis, his expression had settled into something flat and deliberate. "Five hundred grand," he said, as if he were saying it to himself. "That's what we tell 'em. Five hundred. You hearing me?"

Otis blinked. "But he said—"

"Five. Hundred. Grand." Reed's eyes didn't move off Otis until the number sank in.

Otis opened his mouth, closed it, and nodded. "Right. Five hundred."

Along Angeles Crest Highway, a sheriff's car rolled up the road, its blue and red lights blinking. Deputy Murdock, a middle-aged veteran of the force, got out with his gun at the ready. The only sound was the wind whistling through the ravine, carrying with it a sense of dread. He stared at the freshly laid skid marks leading off the pavement, his gaze moving between the ground and the surrounding area. Murdock cautiously made his way toward the ravine, his boots sometimes skidding on the loose dirt, his gun still trained on possible threats. He felt a chill as he saw a car and, beyond that, Deputy Hughes' body. Murdock checked for any signs of life. When he found none, he sat next to the body in silent grief.

Reed crept through the office, his eyes frantically searching Eric's desk. He flicked through invoices and scribbled notes, rifling through documents and tossing them back onto the desk in disarray. Meanwhile, Otis slumbered in the living room, unaware of the chaos in the other room. Eric lay on the floor, eyes half-closed, groaning and wincing in pain. Paige inched toward him and lay next to him, cheek to cheek. "Remember Hawaii? You on that air mattress and the current pulling you out to sea. You said all you could think about was how you didn't want to drown on vacation."

Eric's eyes drifted toward hers. "I made it." His voice was barely there, a dry rasp. "So far."

Suddenly, there was the sound of a car coming. Paige's head popped up. She struggled to get free.

"Mom. Don't."

Reed entered and threw a pen at her. "Listen to the kid. He's obviously a fucking genius." He then went over to Otis and kicked him in the leg, startling him. "Keep 'em quiet," Reed said. Otis placed his gun on his lap as Reed rushed to the window. He saw the deputy's car stop at the bunkhouse and Murdock exit and snoop around.

Murdock saw the uncharacteristic mess. Food remnants, wrapping paper, and more strewn on the ground as well as Paige's lassos. "Hello, anyone around?" Murdock then walked up toward the house.

Reed was at the ready, hiding behind the curtain, motioning Otis to move the family out of the room. And above it all, high on the curtain, hanging on for dear life, was the cat.

Murdock was soon at the front door, knocking, while inside the master bedroom, Otis now had his gun trained on his captives.

"Eric? Paige? Anyone there? It's Tom Murdock."

Otis put his finger to his lips—*Quiet.*

Murdock scanned the family's cars parked in the driveway; nothing seemed out of the ordinary. Reed peered at him from behind the curtain. The cat's tail twitched furiously. Murdock then noticed drag marks and something else on the ground — *blood?*

He crouched lower, his hand drifting toward his holster. The stillness around him felt wrong — too complete, the way silence gets when something's listening to it. His fingers closed around the gun.

Murdock bent closer, and in the polished chrome of the pickup truck's hubcap, a shadow moved — a figure hunched, an arm lifting in a slow, deliberate arc. Murdock's gut clenched as he saw the silhouette advance, something dark and menacing in his grip. Murdock's thumb released the retaining strap securing his gun — leather creaking. Too late.

"Not a good idea," growled Reed, his voice sandpaper-rough. "Get up. Nice and slow."

Murdock rose, feeling Reed's presence like a heat signature on his back. As Reed reached around to seize the deputy's weapon, Murdock pivoted on his heel, arm swinging and connected with Reed's wrist. The gun flew from Reed's grip, tumbling end over end before clattering down the driveway. The deputy yanked his service revolver free, but Reed charged, slamming into Murdock with the force of a freight train, driving him against the truck with a loud thud. The deputy's knuckles cracked against the hood as Reed pinned his gun hand, while delivering a punch into Murdock's solar plexus, forcing the air from his lungs in a painful whoosh. They grappled for the weapon, Reed's whiskey-soured exhalations mixing with the deputy's panicked gasps.

Reed wrenched Murdock's wrist until the gun clattered across the hood. Off balance, Reed clutched at the antenna to steady himself. The metal rod bowed under his weight. Choking for air, but not finished, Murdock drove a short savage hook into Reed's ribs. Reed grunted — and let go of the antenna; it snapped upright, lashing across his eyes. "Jesus, fuck!" Reed howled. Blinded and furious, he shoved the antenna away, unintentionally driving its tip into Murdock's eye socket. The deputy's hold on Reed instantly went slack, allowing Reed to seize Murdock's skull in a vise-like grip between his palms and thrust it down hard, driving the antenna deeper into Murdock's skull. The deputy's body went limp, sliding down the hood's polished surface as the metal rod snapped back, vibrating with a metallic twang. Something wet and gelatinous — the deputy's eyeball — arcing through the air.

Back in the house, Otis kicked the side of a table after Reed gave him his next task. "Why the hell do I always have to do the dirty work?" Otis whined.

Reed was holding a bag of frozen peas over his eye. "Because you're good at it. Now get out there and get rid of him."

"And how the hell do I hide a police car?"

"Bury it… paint it… put it in the barn… figure it out. I don't give a shit… just do it."

Otis stomped toward the door, mumbling, "Always me, like I'm some kinda fucking slave. One day…"

"And stop your fucking mumbling."

Reed then flung open the door to the bedroom. The Martins startled. "Looks like you won't be getting rescued today," he said.

Otis stepped out of the front door, plucked a kumquat from the tree, then stopped. The deputy's eyeball hung there among the branches, still wet and glistening. He popped the fruit in his mouth, glancing at the eyeball dangling and smirked. "What you are you looking at?" He swatted it hard, sending it flying into the nearby foliage.

Otis then spotted a gardening cart near the side of the house, overflowing with terracotta pots. Cursing under his breath, he dumped them onto the ground with a series of hollow cracks and dragged the cart around front. Murdock's body proved heavier than expected — dead weight in the most literal sense — as Otis struggled to heave the corpse into the cart. The dead man's legs were draped over the back end. As Otis walked around to grab the handle, one of Murdock's legs brushed against his and slid off the side. He kicked it back. "Asshole!" Otis then wheeled the jangling cart down to the bunkhouse with him slipping on some pebbles that rolled underfoot. He caught himself and then moved forward again. "Fuck this shit!"

At the bunkhouse, Otis wrestled Murdock's corpse into the trunk of the Sheriff's car, sweat beading on his forehead and soaking through his armpits. The body flopped like a half-empty sandbag, arms twisting at unnatural angles. "Always me," he muttered through clenched teeth, "while he just sits around and plays Mr. king-a-the-hill with his fucking frozen peas." Otis slammed the trunk shut, his fingers leaving smudges on the polished black metal. "One day, he'll be sorry."

He climbed into the driver's seat. A shotgun was securely locked between the seats; he tugged at it, fumbled with the special locking mechanism but it wouldn't give. "Fucking shotgun. Go fuck yourself."

He fired up the engine and drove into the barn. Otis then got out and slammed the car door, hard enough that the suspension shuddered. His foot connected with the driver's side door, leaving a dent shaped like the toe of his boot. "I hope he stinks up your fucking trunk bad enough to melt your fucking tires," he growled. When done, Otis pulled the creaking barn door closed, then froze at the sound of tires on gravel. Another car. He ducked behind a stack of hay bales, heart hammering against his ribs.

CHAPTER FIVE

WINE, BREAD, AND THE TWO STOOGES

Otis pressed his back against the hay bales and held his breath. The tires crunched to a stop. A car door slammed. Then another. He waited, eyes squeezed shut like that might help, before finally risking a peek around the edge of the bales.

Garvey stepped out, trailed by Travis, a small but bulky man in his mid-30s with a cocky air of superiority, and Bonnet, a grinning prankster, both of them carrying jumbo cups of soda.

Relieved, Otis came out of hiding. "Hey, Garvey! You made it."

"Of course I made it. I'm here."

The passenger door swung open and out tumbled Cindy, her half-smoked cigarette dangling from her mouth. She fixed Otis with a hard stare.

"Who the hell is that?" asked Otis.

"My new old lady."

Otis shook his head, eyes darting nervously as he led them toward the house. "I don't think Reed's gonna like this. Uh, uh. Not good." His voice dropped to a mutter with each step up the path. "He don't like surprises. Nope. Not good."

Up at the house, Reed was at Eric's computer desk with Paige who had her hands tied behind her. He pointed at different people in photographs. "Who's that?"

"The bank president, Mr. Arquette."

"And this one?"

"Loan officer, Mrs. Reade."

Reed smirked at the coincidence of sharing a name with someone in banking. He jabbed his finger toward the computer screen. "Now show me how to run this thing. How do I turn it on?"

"That button."

"Which button?"

"That one."

"Which fucking button?"

"How the hell can I show you which button with my hands tied?"

Otis opened the front door and called out, "They're here."

Reed grabbed hold of Paige and shoved her back into the master bedroom where he retied her feet. He then strode into the living room, a grin spreading across his face at the sight of his buddies casing the joint — until his eyes locked on Cindy. His smile vanished. "Whoa, whoa. What the hell is that broad doing here?"

"Broad?" said Cindy. "Who the hell says broad? What are you like a hundred years old or something?" She smacked Garvey's arm. "Did you hear what that asshole called me?"

"Shut up," said Garvey.

Cindy gave him a dirty look then pointed to Reed. "You better watch who you're calling a broad, fuckface."

Reed eyed her carefully as Garvey said, "This is Cindy. She won't get in the way."

"She's already in the way. Put her on a leash."

"Try it, you mother..." urged Cindy, looking for a fight.

"Hey, hey... go make yourself useful. Go get us some food," said Garvey, trying to quell the impending brawl.

"I'm not your fucking maid."

Cindy caught Garvey's warning glare, flipped Reed the bird behind his back, then stomped toward the kitchen with her cigarette parked at the corner of her mouth and mumbling to herself, "Fucking men. Always with their fucking orders. One day." They could see her as she stomped around the kitchen, loudly flinging open various cabinets, pretending she was looking for something... anything resembling what they might want to eat.

Travis dropped into an armchair and sank back into the plush upholstery with a grunt of approval, running his palm along the armrest like he was pricing it. Bonnet circled the room more slowly, hands in his pockets, his eyes moving across the shelves and side tables with the quiet, practiced attention of a man taking inventory. He paused at a side table, lifted a small decorative compass — the kind that sits in a leather case — turned it over once, and slipped it into his pants pocket. A moment later his fingers closed around a silver money clip sitting next to a stack of mail. That went into the other pocket. Travis glanced over, clocked it. He'd seen this before.

"So, what the hell's going on?" Garvey demanded.

"I got a guy in the back that has a bank," Reed said, "with... ah... five hundred grand waiting for us to collect."

"Damn!" said Garvey as Travis and Bonnet perked up.

Otis jerked his head quizzically at Reed, about to open his mouth, but Reed shot him a look —*keep your mouth shut.*

"I ain't cooking any of this shit, I can tell ya that," Cindy yelled back at them.

Garvey scoffed at Reed's words and shook his head. "Yeah, well there's a catch now ain't there?"

Reed's face suddenly lost its composure. His brow furrowed, his lips tightened.

"What, you don't know the highway patrol is up and down the interstate and cops checking IDs at every turn? Fucking roadblocks all over the place," reported Garvey.

In the bedroom, Paige and Adam sat on the floor next to Eric. The door was open so they could hear Otis scream, "Roadblocks? Now, what the fuck we gonna do? I told you we shoulda got out when we had the chance."

Reed pounced on Otis, grabbed him by the shirt and smacked him against the side of his head, so hard it bounced off the wall. "Listen, moron. This deal's gonna make it all worthwhile. You think I'd let them lock me up again?" Otis clutched his head to protect against another slamming. Reed paced, sweating at the very thought of prison. Now a haunted man, his eyes wild and desperate. "I ain't ever going back. Every day is like a week. Every week a year. Then another and another. Well, fuck that!"

Cindy watched — nervous *and* excited; she and Garvey exchanged concerned glances.

Reed slowed his pace and stopped in front of Otis. The desperate voice inside him quieted. He took a moment to compose himself then leaned closer and whispered through clenched teeth, "You got that?"

"Yeah, Reed, I got it. I got it. Ain't gonna happen."

"You *all* got that? This is a fucking gold mine. You in or out?"

"Yeah, Reed, sure, piece a cake," said Garvey, rattled by Reed's behavior but still keen to make some quick cash from an easy source.

Cindy abandoned the kitchen, trailing cigarette ash like breadcrumbs behind her, as she wandered down the hallway pushing open doors to inspect what lay beyond. Behind her, dashing past, was the cat. She came to the master bedroom where she looked in on the hostages, zeroing in on Paige. She flicked open a switchblade with a practiced snap of her wrist, the blade catching the light as she approached. Moments later, Cindy returned to the living room with Paige, whose hands were now tied in front of her with a frayed rope that cut into her wrists. The men all stared, their faces a mix of surprise and anticipation. "I told ya I wasn't cooking," Cindy announced, her voice raspy from cigarettes.

She pushed Paige into the kitchen with a sharp jab between the shoulder blades, sending her stumbling against the counter. Cindy's eyes narrowed when she spotted the wooden knife holder. She snatched it, sliding her fingers over the handles before yanking out a gleaming chef's knife. "You'd better fix something nice, honey," she said, testing the blade's edge with her thumb, "they're hungry."

Paige stretched out her hands, expecting to be untied. "Only my husband gets to call me honey."

Cindy ignored Paige's outstretched hands and exhaled cigarette smoke in her direction. "How about I call you 'bitch'?"

"How about I call you 'broad'?" was Paige's quick retort.

Cindy responded with a quirky smile and a flicker of ash dropped to the floor. "What's your name?"

"Paige."

"I'm Cindy."

Cindy glanced out at Reed as Paige took out boxes of spaghetti and stuffed energy bars in her pocket. "So, Reed, you through with your little tantrum or what?"

"Shut the fuck up, broad."

"Hey Garvey, you'd better tell him to talk nice to me or I'll get her to poison his fucking food."

"Just cook something up, already," Garvey shouted back.

Reed glanced over at Otis. "Otis, tell me, who's watching the kid and the yuppie?"

Cindy flung a bag of tortilla chips onto the coffee table near where the men were sitting. She was still holding onto the knife holder. "Appetizers."

"I'm getting closet-phobia in that room, you know," Otis complained.

"Check 'em anyway."

Otis stormed out, mumbling.

In the kitchen, Paige spotted the cat's empty food dish in the far corner. Despite her trembling fingers, she found a tin of food in the cupboard, wrestled the lid off, and upended the whole glistening mass into the bowl with a wet plop.

When the men's dinner was ready, the gang sat at the dining table and Reed passed around a wine bottle. Paige and Adam were relegated to a corner, like kids at a grown-up event, where they silently picked at their food with plastic forks. They alternately looked at one another and then away from their captors. When Adam noticed an energy bar poking up from Paige's pocket, he stuffed it back down. She pursed her lips into a tense smile then spotted the cat make a dash to the food bowl.

Paige kept her eyes on her plate but she was sizing up the gang. Reed needed to be the smartest man in the room. Otis needed Reed to love him. Garvey needed the money more than he needed Reed. She didn't know yet what to do with any of that information, but she was keeping score.

Reed took a sloppy gulp of wine and planted the glass on the table. "Good stuff." The men shoveled in the spaghetti but Cindy ate more conservatively between puffs of her ever-present cigarette.

Otis said to Paige, "This is good too. You make the sauce yourself?"

"Yeah," she said, barely able to stomach the conversation.

"Yeah, Mom always made it fresh too." Reed scowled at Otis then waved the empty bread basket at Paige. She took it and stepped into the kitchen to fetch more. When she returned, she plopped the bread in front of Reed and went back to her corner with Adam. Otis grabbed a piece first and Reed knocked his hand away. "What?" said Otis.

"Wait your turn."

"God, it's just a fucking piece of bread."

Reed took his piece, then Otis grabbed a hunk and asked Paige, "You make the bread too or is it store-bought?"

Reed pounded his fork on the table. "What are you... Suzie Homemaker or something?"

"What's with you guys?" asked Cindy. "It's like listening to the two Stooges."

Travis interrupted, "There was three of them."

Cindy glared at him and stated the obvious. "But there's only two of 'em here."

Bonnet began to imitate the third Stooge, Curly, from one of their skits. "Moe, Larry... the cheese. Moe, Larry... the cheese." Otis laughed so hard that he spat spaghetti all over himself. He then slid the Parmesan to Bonnet.

"Can we cut this shit?" barked Garvey. He then turned to Reed. "How we gonna do the bank?"

Reed snapped his fingers at Otis and pointed to Paige and Adam. "Get 'em outta here."

Adam announced, "I have to go to the bathroom."

Otis stood and shoveled in one more mouthful as Reed waited for them to leave. Once they were out of the room, Reed turned to Garvey. "We do it tomorrow morning. And the roadblocks aren't a problem. The banker will drive us right through."

Otis listened to the men's conversation as he stood at the door outside the guest bathroom where he waited for Adam to finish up. "Hurry up in there." He peeked into Adam's bedroom and spied the computer with its cool screen saver just as Adam exited the bathroom. "That's a neat thing on your computer, kid."

Adam's eyes widened as an idea suddenly took shape. "Want to see something awesome?" He beckoned Otis into the room with a conspiratorial nod. Otis' eyes widened at the computer setup, the posters, the collectibles lining the shelves. While Otis was distracted by the teenage treasures, Adam slid into his desk chair and woke up the computer with a quick tap.

Nestled on the bed, between two pillows, was the cat. It slinked back, disappearing behind the pillows.

"You sure your boss won't get mad?" Adam asked.

Otis joined Adam at the computer. "That's not my boss, that's my brother," he said, not quite meeting Adam's eyes.

"Your brother treats you like that?"

Otis awkwardly tried to shift the conversation. "Well... hey, come on, show me." Adam pulled up a game, and Otis' eyes lit up as he took in the amazing graphics. "Wow! That's cool!" he said.

Adam glanced at the door to make sure no one was coming. "I bet you'd be good at it." He indicated the joystick. "Here, use this."

Otis took the joystick and pretended he knew what he was doing before declaring, "Now I gotta take a piss. No funny business while I'm gone, okay?"

"Sure."

As Otis left the room, Adam instantly launched a messaging app. He frantically typed a text message to a friend while listening for the bathroom door.

"No cheatin'," Otis called out.

Adam tapped his foot impatiently as he waited for a reply. He then regained composure when he heard the toilet flushing. Otis re-entered and grabbed the joystick. "I had one of these when I was a kid. Haven't played in a while. Reed won't let me. Says I'm too old."

They played the game just long enough so no one would become suspicious of their absence, but when he came back to the living room, Otis was still imitating the sounds of the computer game.

The gang was huddled over photos of the bank from Eric's desk. Cindy watched from her perch on Garvey's knee and suppressed a yawn. Her head swiveled as she heard a faint ping coming from where the bedrooms were. She scampered off to investigate, her shoes slapping against the hardwood floor.

As she walked down the hallway, she heard another ping coming from Adam's bedroom. Cindy turned, entered the room and noticed his computer was turned on and the messaging app icon with a small "2" beneath it. She clicked it, and two messages popped up in a window. "Hey, you better see this," she called out.

When Reed arrived, Cindy pointed at the messages from MarvelousMarci:

"Called back 2X. hostages? weirdos? Come on!"

"if you didn't want to see me 2night, u shoulda just said so!"

Reed stared at the screen, blood boiling. A vein throbbed at his temple like a trapped worm beneath his skin. His hands became a tornado of destruction as he swept the computer off the desk with a crash that sent plastic shards skittering across the floor. He yanked cords from their sockets with such force that sparks flew. Like a rabid animal, he tore through the house furiously dismantling any phone or device that could have been a source of rescue. The others shot to their feet, chair legs clawing at the hardwood floor. Reed's breath came in bull-like snorts as he stormed into the master bedroom where Paige and Adam cowered. Otis hung back in the doorway with the others and winced, his heart pounding as he shifted his feet nervously and wrung his hands, knowing what was coming.

Paige screamed as Reed approached. "Stop!"

Reed threw Adam onto the bed then slapped Paige hard across the face. Cindy's jaw tightened. The men watched, amused. Adam's glasses flew off. Paige pressed her tongue against the inside of her cheek where it had caught her teeth, tasting blood, her eyes going straight to Adam to make sure he was alright. Reed then grabbed Adam by the neck. "You little four-eyed creep. You send messages thinking we're too stupid to notice?"

Otis said, "Wha... what'd he do?"

"And you, shit-for-brains. You were supposed to keep your fucking eyes on him." Reed smacked Adam again.

Paige struggled against her ropes. "Stop. Please stop."

Eric awoke to the sight of the intruders and was filled with a sensation of powerlessness. But when he saw his ravaged loved ones, he tried to stand, only to be met by a swift kick from Reed. Reed then ordered Travis and Bonnet, "Lock 'em in the laundry room... in the back." They looked to Garvey for their marching orders. He gave them a nod.

CHAPTER SIX

DIRTY LAUNDRY AND BRIGHT-EYED RACCOONS

The thud of the laundry room door closing and the scrape of wire looped around the doorknob binding it shut were still fading when Reed turned his attention to Otis. He was more composed now, but the calm on his face was the kind that preceded something worse. He crossed the living room toward his brother, who cringed before Reed had even opened his mouth.

"You know, Otis, I do all the thinking so we can get somewhere in this life and you're just fucking it up. You let the kid send a message to his girlfriend."

"How the hell could he do that? I was with him the whole time."

"You tell me."

Otis spoke low, trying to both weasel out of it and save face in front of the other men. "Come on, Reed, we got enough money now. Let's just get outta here. These people are making you cuckoo or something."

Reed glowered at him. "Don't you ever fucking say that to me again or I'll fucking wring your scrawny neck so you squirt blood out your asshole. Tell you what — you don't like it here? Then leave. Get the fuck out. See how far you get."

Otis cowered away, trembling at the thought of going it alone. "Ah, come on, Reed, we're family. You know you need me. You're smarter, but who's always been there for you, huh?"

Reed could feel the fear radiating off Otis and found a sick pleasure in it before he finally relented. "All right, if you wanna stay... but only because you're my brother."

"Okay. I'll stay, but only because you need me," Otis said, trying to sound braver than he felt.

Reed grabbed a bottle of whiskey and plopped into a chair.

Otis stood where he was for a moment, his jaw working like he might say something else. He didn't. His shoulders dropped a couple of inches and he let out a long, slow breath through his nose.

Cindy saw it. She went over and put a hand on his shoulder. "Come on, Otis, let's get some fresh air."

They stood on the front porch where Cindy took a hit from a joint then passed it to Otis who took several big draws before admitting, "He gets so damn mad at everything."

"Don't worry, Otis. After we get the money, everything's going to be just fine. You'll see."

Cindy watched him settle, then said, easy and offhand, "So what's Reed so worked up about anyway? Half a million's not nothing."

"Yeah." Otis took another long draw and held it. "Well, it's more than that."

Cindy exhaled slowly. "Oh? How much more?"

"Over a million." He shook his head like he still couldn't believe it. "Reed almost shit when he heard it. Wow."

Cindy let out a low whistle and handed the joint back to him. "Well, damn," she said, like it was mildly interesting news about someone else's money. She took a slow drag and looked out at the dark tree line, giving him nothing — just a woman killing time on a porch. But behind that, the numbers were already moving.

"Man, I got me the munchies. Gotta get something to eat." Otis gently patted Cindy on the back. "Thanks, Cindy. You're okay," he said, as he retreated into the house.

Cindy noticed Garvey and Reed through the window and surreptitiously tilted her chin toward the porch and signaled for Garvey to come outside. A few moments later, he joined her. "So how long have you known this Reed? And do you trust him?" she asked.

Garvey grabbed her joint and took a hit. "You got something to say? Say it."

"Listen, dickhead, you can get away with talking shit to me in front of the others but this is you and me standing here."

"Okay. Calm down. We did time together. He always had my back."

"Maybe he had your back then so he can pull shit behind it now."

"What the fuck are you talking about?"

From the living room, Reed could see Garvey and Cindy chatting. When Garvey looked back through the window at Reed, he noticed him chuckling at something on the television.

"That lying greedy pig," said Garvey.

"What are you gonna do?"

"I'm gonna go in there and cut his fucking nuts off."

"Oh, that's real smart. Wait till after. Then we take it all."

"This is why I keep you around." He grabbed Cindy and kissed her hard.

When he came up for air, Cindy said, "You don't keep me around. I stick around." She pressed a finger into his chest. "*I'll* cut his nuts off."

Garvey smiled and tapped her earring, the one shaped like a question mark. "I knew this was perfect for you. Always thinking."

Travis and Bonnet heard banging and cries coming from the laundry room. "Let us out!" shouted Paige. "We need to use the bathroom, please!" Travis unwound the wire that had been keeping the door secured and opened it up. Paige immediately began to move past him, but he held his arm out for her to stay put. "Please, let us use the bathroom," she said again.

Travis glanced at Bonnet and he nodded. "Make it quick," he said.

Adam helped Paige with Eric to the doorway but Bonnet pushed Adam back inside.

The bathroom, to where they were directed, was a mess. The toilet seat was down and peed on, soap and grime all over the sink, like it was some gas station restroom that hadn't seen a janitor in ages. Paige held Eric back from the toilet. She grabbed paper towels and a cleaning solution from under the sink. And when she uncapped the bottle, she was hit by a whiff of ammonia. Good. Finally some luck, she thought. She turned to Eric. "Quick, take off your pants."

Eric hesitated then did it and dropped them to the floor. She poured the cleaner onto the crotch of his pants. He stared, confused, and repulsed by the odor. Paige then opened the door and thrust Eric's pants inches from the men's faces.

"What the fuck?!" screamed Travis as he recoiled from the door frame.

"He didn't make it to the toilet. Now he needs a shower."

Bonnet glanced in and saw Eric standing in the shower looking like a drooped flower. "Yeah." He pulled the door shut with a slam.

Paige turned on the shower and whispered, "All I need is five minutes."

"What are you doing?"

"Bunkhouse phone."

"Too dangerous."

"Trust me."

Paige went to the window and crawled out. But standing just outside the house, near the corner of the porch, was Cindy smoking a cigarette. She became distracted by the sound of the bathroom window opening and saw Paige's leg and butt exiting. She watched, amused, then opened the front door and popped her head in.

"Hey, fuckface!" she shouted to Reed. "You got another hostage problem."

That ended Paige's escapade. In just a few minutes, she found herself back in the laundry room with Eric and Adam, all with their hands tied behind them. Eric was in his underwear, soaked, his legs bruised and swelling, while Adam had a black eye. Paige had a dark bruise on her cheek from the smack Reed gave her.

They heard Travis and Bonnet chatting outside the door. "I'd love to tap that ass," said Travis, staring at the door, his eyes glistening. He looked down the hallway to see if anyone else was present then reached for the doorknob.

Bonnet gave him a light smack on his arm. "Garvey said no fucking around on the job. Let's get back."

Their footsteps trailed off down the hallway.

Later, Reed took up the entire bed in the master bedroom with his arms and legs spread out as if he had been tied to the bedposts. Otis was curled into the fetal position, lying on a half-made bed in Adam's room. And Garvey and Cindy were entwined under the sheets, tucked in close, in Grandpa Billy's room. The rest of the house had gone semi-quiet, with Travis and Bonnet taking over the living room's recliner and sofa, the tempo of their snores battling it out.

In the laundry room, Adam sat against the door and Paige sat next to Eric, whose head was back as vacant eyes looked to the ceiling. Paige's head was bowed as she sobbed. "I'm so sorry."

Eric rolled his head to kiss her on the cheek. "Don't blame yourself."

Paige's tears dripped to the floor where she watched them puddle on the cracked flooring. She stayed there a moment, just long enough to let the grief be what it was. Then something shifted behind her eyes — a decision, not a feeling — and she lifted her head.

Her swollen eyes darted from the small porcelain sink to the floorboards underneath, then finally settled on Adam's slumped figure in the corner. "Adam... Adam," she whispered, her voice hoarse from crying. He lifted his head slowly, revealing bloodshot eyes and a face etched with exhaustion. "Have you heard anything out there?" He shook his head "no," the movement barely perceptible in the dim light filtering through the laundry room window. "You have to get your hands in front of you — now." Her words hung in the stale air between them as Adam stared back blankly, his mind clearly fogged by fear. "Slide your hands down the back of your legs until you can get them in front of you," she explained, demonstrating the motion with her own bound wrists. "Understand?"

Now he got it. Adam nodded. He worked his hands until they were in front of him.

"Come over and untie us. Be quiet."

Adam untied their hands then Paige untied his. She quietly slid out a box of laundry cleaners, revealing warped floorboards from an unfortunate water leak.

"What's going on?" Adam asked.

Eric looked at the floorboards then saw Paige's desperation. It didn't take long for him to realize what she was doing. He grabbed an old bath towel, handed it to Adam and nodded toward the bottom of the door. Adam stuffed it along the bottom frame.

Paige looked around the room for something to use. Eric said, "Check the closet." She opened the door to the small broom closet and spotted a pair of gardening gloves on a shelf and underneath them, a pair of gardening shears. She grabbed the shears and knelt at the sink.

"No. Let Adam do it," Eric said, which surprised Adam. "Think you can get through?" Eric asked. Adam looked over at the floorboards and nodded.

He surveyed the warped floorboards, noting the darkened edges where moisture had seeped in over time. "Dad, throw me those big towels," he said, his voice barely above a whisper. Eric winced as he reached for the stack of old bath towels, tossing them across the cramped space. Paige handed Adam the garden shears — rusty at the hinge but still sharp enough along the blades — then extracted a pair of Eric's khaki work pants from the overflowing hamper, the fabric still bearing traces of red clay from the property. She pressed her ear against the door, listening for any movement while Adam laid the towels in overlapping layers across the target area. With a deep breath, he slipped his hands beneath them and began working the shears into the seam between planks, feeling the old wood splinter and give way beneath each twist of his wrists.

Eric struggled to put on the pants while wincing in pain. "You two go. I'll never make it."

"We're not leaving you," Paige whispered back in disbelief to his suggestion. She found a bed sheet in the hamper and tore it into strips that she wrapped around Eric's ribs. "So suck it up." He mustered a weak smile.

Adam finally broke through. He kept at it until the hole was big enough to crawl through. The room light shone down through the hole and Paige and Adam looked down into the crawlspace. A family of raccoons stared up at them. They both startled at the unexpected sight.

"Shit," whispered Paige.

"What's wrong?" Eric asked.

"Raccoons," said Adam.

"So?"

Paige and Adam looked back down and saw the adults bare their teeth. She grabbed a towel and threw it down at them. The babies scattered but the adults stood their ground.

"I'll go first, Mom. I'll get them to move."

"Be careful."

Adam began lowering himself while Paige tried to see what the raccoons were doing. One of them grabbed a hold of Adam's leg. He stifled a scream and tried to shake it off.

"Oh my God, rabies," said Paige. "Don't let him bite."

The raccoon wouldn't budge. Adam used his other foot to push it off. The raccoon hissed and then ran off, allowing

Adam to drop down. "Clear," he called back up. Paige helped Eric down the hole as Adam reached up from below. She then eased herself down.

In the crawlspace, a glimpse of early sun barely shone in from the house skirting. A section had been pulled away. Paige and Adam crouched low in the restricted space as they struggled to move Eric along.

Then out of nowhere, there was Grandpa Billy, sitting up against a pillar, very much alive, although dirty and disoriented. He had a strange, dazed look on his face and a young raccoon on his lap. A trail of scuff marks in the dirt led back toward the far end of the house — looked like he'd dragged himself the whole way. Then again, Otis had been told to get rid of him. This was probably his version of it.

Shocked, Paige whispered, "Dad!"

"Grandpa!"

Grandpa slurred loudly, "Who are you?"

Paige pressed her index finger against her lips, silencing Grandpa before rushing to his side and waving the raccoon away. She froze, head tilted toward the ceiling, listening for any creaks or footsteps above — nothing. Meanwhile, Grandpa seemed oblivious to their danger, his weathered hands making gentle beckoning motions toward the corner where the little creature had disappeared.

"Dad, it's me. How did you get here?"

"Who cares?!" Eric blurted out.

"Come on, Mom… Grandpa, let's go."

"What about Hannah-Banana?" Grandpa reached out for the little raccoon that had now scampered away as Paige helped him to his knees and Adam helped Eric.

"We have to go," she said.

CHAPTER SEVEN
HEADS WILL ROLL

The foursome struggled out from under the house, their clothes caked with dirt and cobwebs, and headed down the driveway toward the bunkhouse. The first rays of dawn painted the sky a pale orange, casting long shadows across the property, and the main house windows glowed above them like watching eyes. Eric's weight dragged between them, and the gravel crunched loud enough under their feet to make Paige wince with every step. Grandpa, his white hair disheveled and eyes gleaming with misplaced excitement, took a deep wheezing breath and announced with military bravado, "I love the smell of napalm in the morning."

Paige, her face tense with worry, quickly clamped her hand over his chapped lips. "Enemy on our six," she whispered, her eyes darting toward the main house.

Grandpa's expression shifted instantly from jovial to alert, his spine straightening, jaw set, eyes scanning the perimeter like the veteran he once was. Just then, the yellow porch light flickered on. Paige's pulse shot up and her stomach knotted as she grabbed Grandpa's arm and jerked her head toward the dense pine trees. "This way."

"What about the phone?" asked Adam.

"No time." Paige led them deeper into the woods.

Inside the Martin house, Otis stood at the entrance of the laundry room, a box of cereal and bowls jostling in his hands. His face was a mask of shock as he looked in and found it empty. He let out a horrid scream that echoed down the hallway, causing others to come running.

"That's it!" Reed proclaimed, as he spotted the torn-up flooring.

"They're carrying half a dead man." Garvey tried to reassure him.

"All they need is to get to a phone. We need him alive."

The gang sprinted down the driveway, scanning the area for any sign of the escapees. After quickly checking in around the bunkhouse, Reed cut the phone line. He then instructed Travis and Bonnet, "Go back and look around the main house. Garvey and me will check between here and the main road. Otis, you and... *her* go that way."

They headed off in different directions.

Deep in the woods, Eric's legs buckled beneath him. He sank to the ground with a muffled groan. "We leave no man behind," Grandpa whispered, his eyes darting between the trees. Adam looped his arm under his father's shoulder and hoisted him upright. They pressed forward, leaving only crushed leaves in their wake.

Travis and Bonnet looked under and around the house and cars. Otis and Cindy, well-armed, scanned the area as they moved through the woods. A twig snapped. Cindy spun around with her gun — aiming it right at Otis. He was holding onto a branch that was slightly broken. She lowered her gun. "Jesus, Otis!"

"See, this is how you tell if they came this way, if the branch is broken."

"Well, did they come this way?"

"I don't know. I just wanted to show you how you could tell. Learned it in the Boy Scouts."

"They actually let you become a Boy Scout? Oh...okay." She moved off, leaving Otis to examine the flora.

Reed and Garvey drove one dirt road after another, spotting nothing but trees, bushes and one frightened deer. Garvey pretended to take a potshot at it.

Finally, Paige spotted the entrance to a small, shallow cave. They made their way to it, and once inside, Adam moved some old beer cans and other party debris to the side, then helped his mother lower his father to the ground. Eric groaned in pain. "Easy," she said. Eric coughed up a bit of blood.

"Come on, Dad." Adam tried to encourage him.

Paige then helped her father settle in. As he moved to sit down, he said to Eric, "Stay awake, soldier, that's an order. I'll take the first watch."

"What's with Grandpa?" Adam asked.

"I think he had a minor stroke."

"What are we gonna do?"

Paige put her hand on Adam's arm. "I have to get to a phone."

"The bunkhouse?"

Eric coughed again then dropped into unconsciousness.

"It'll take longer but it'll be safer for me to get to the main road."

"Call in the cavalry!" Grandpa shouted.

"But Mom…"

"Don't worry, I know these woods better than they do. Take care of your father." She pulled out the energy bars and gave them to Adam. "Try to keep Grandpa quiet." Paige gave Adam and Eric a quick kiss before spotting Grandpa looking toward the cave entrance and tearing up.

"Hannah-Banana. I'll miss ya, buddy," said Grandpa.

Somewhere in the woods, Cindy looked back for Otis and tripped on something solid but yielding beneath a pile of leaves. Her boot had caught on Glen's stiffening arm, now waxy in the filtered morning light. She stumbled backward and spotted another mound of disturbed dirt a few feet away, then another beyond that, both bulging unnaturally against the earth. She kicked away the hasty covering to reveal faces frozen in terror, eyes clouded and skin mottled with purple-black blotches where blood had pooled. The metallic stench of death mixed with loamy earth hit her nostrils. She stared wide-eyed, her throat constricting as acid rose in her stomach.

Suddenly, Otis crashed through the underbrush behind her, his heavy breathing cutting through the silence before catching in his throat as he took in the grotesque tableau.

"No one said anything about dead people all over the place," she hissed, as she gestured wildly at the corpses. "We came to rob a bank, not fucking kill everyone in sight." Otis backed away, his face draining of color, sweat beading along his receding hairline despite the morning chill. Cindy advanced on him, jabbing her finger into his chest. "What's with you and that brother of yours? Are you fucking lunatics?"

Cindy looked back at the bodies. "I'm not taking the rap for this."

Otis stepped back from Cindy's fury, his heel landing on something unnatural. Unnaturally soft yet firm — the severed hands. His body convulsed before his mind could process why, jerking the shotgun. The blast tore through the morning stillness. A load of pellets spat from the barrel and bits of flesh shot up from one of the severed hands he hit. One pellet ricocheted and caught Cindy's prized earring, the question mark, and tore it clean off. She touched her ear in shock, blood trickling down her neck. "What the fuck!" she screamed, and bolted toward the trees. Otis flung the shotgun away and ran in the opposite direction.

Along her route, Paige heard the gunshot crack. Then she saw it — the shotgun tumbling through the air, and both Otis and Cindy scattering.

Paige ran over and checked Otis' shotgun. It was now empty, so she left it where she found it. She then discovered the mangled bodies. "Oh my God." She leaned back against a tree and closed her eyes — all her friends, people who'd sat at her table, eating, laughing, having a good time. Now dead in the woods because of a her party. She pressed her head back against the tree, the rough bark scraping her scalp. She breathed. Then it dawned on her — "Margie."

Paige stumbled around looking for Margie. Her eyes quickly darted from tree to tree, looking for any signs of life. All she could see were dark shadows and dull colors in the thick of the forest. The only sound was Paige's own breathing, which was coming in fast, shallow breaths. Her heart thumped loud and heavy. Then her gaze fell on Margie's body, propped up against a tree with her eyes open. "Margie?" There were small red marks across her forehead and neck and her clothes were ripped, evidence of the violence done to her. Paige's hands were shaking as she gently touched Margie's body to see if there was any life left in her. Then Margie's head dropped off. Paige jumped back, then her legs weakened, so much so that she dropped to the ground.

Reed's car rattled down the dirt road with him hunched over the steering wheel and Garvey bracing himself against the dashboard as he scanned the trees. Suddenly, Cindy burst from the underbrush ahead, sprinting toward them. Reed's knuckles whitened on the wheel as he and Garvey locked eyes in bewilderment. "Where the hell is she going?" Reed asked.

Garvey screamed at Cindy, "Hey, hey, what happened?" Cindy ignored him and kicked it into high gear.

Reed slammed on the brakes and then backed up fast to parallel her. She was on Reed's side, so Garvey screamed over Reed to her. "Stop running, goddammit."

Her eyes darted between the road and Reed. "I'm not taking the rap for all those bodies."

"What bodies?"

She looked at Reed and said, "He's fucking crazy."

Garvey eyed Reed. "What bodies?!"

The car engine roared as Reed slammed down on the gas pedal. His eyes went wild, his face twisted in anger. His gaze was fully focused on Cindy, unblinking as he maneuvered the car to hit her. Garvey was screaming at him to stop as his hand grabbed at Reed's and struggled to take control of the wheel. The car darted around, almost seeming to dance with Cindy as Reed swatted and punched at Garvey. Cindy looked over her shoulder and saw the men battling it out. Her high-pitched screams filled the air as her feet pounded the ground. The car spun 180, then stopped abruptly, now facing Cindy. Reed gunned the engine again.

Cindy fumbled for the pistol tucked into her waistband. The hammer snagged on her pants; she gave it a hard pull, causing the weapon to slip out of her hand and clatter to the dirt. She dove after it, fingers closing around the grip as she rolled onto her back and squeezed the trigger. The windshield erupted in a spiderweb of cracks as Reed jerked the wheel. The car fishtailed wildly before launching over the roadside embankment, its nose plunging into the soft earth at a near-vertical angle, like some bizarre monument marking an invisible grave. Cindy didn't wait to see more — she was already gone, legs pumping, lungs burning.

It took a moment before either door opened. Then Garvey's door swung out, and he half-climbed, half-fell onto the tilted ground, spitting dirt and grabbing at the car to pull himself upright. Reed came out the other side, dragging himself up the embankment on his hands and knees, his shirt torn and one sleeve hanging by a thread. They stood at the roadside, breathing hard, blood on both their faces from the windshield glass.

Before Garvey could catch his breath, Reed charged at him, leg cocked back for a vicious kick. Garvey caught the boot mid-swing and yanked hard, sending Reed sprawling onto his back. "Have you lost your goddamn mind?" Garvey yelled with disbelief as he stared down Reed. "STOP!"

It wasn't happening. Reed got up and they started beating on one another — two beat-up men on a dirt road, both already half-wrecked, throwing punches that landed slower and slower as their legs gave out. Reed's ribs were cracked from the crash and every swing cost him; Garvey's right eye was swelling shut but he kept swinging anyway, both of them too stubborn and too stupid to stop until Reed finally pulled his gun and cocked the hammer. Garvey, his heart pounding into his throat, put his hands out in front of him. "Jesus Christ! I thought we came here to rob a bank. Will you fucking stop?"

Reed's eyes were bulged out as he seethed but that one word — bank — did the trick. He eased up.

Garvey exhaled with relief and suggested, "Let's go find your bank guy, okay?"

"Yeah...okay," said Reed, who was out of breath and out of other options.

Garvey glanced once down the road where Cindy had disappeared, long enough to know she wasn't coming back, then they moved off injured and limping.

In another area, a haggard Otis was dazed, wandering, lost, and bumping into tree limbs and bushes. His clothes were torn and dirtied as if he had been making his way through the woods for days. "I didn't kill them. I didn't even know they was dead. It's not my fault." He looked around. "Same fucking trees everywhere." He swatted wildly at bugs buzzing his head. "Fucking bugs, will you get the fuck away from me, you little fucks." The only other sound was the soft thuds of Otis' footsteps as he stumbled around in circles.

Paige, still an emotional wreck after seeing her dead friends, spotted Travis and Bonnet near the front of the bunkhouse.

"I'll try to find Reed and Garvey," said Bonnet. "You keep looking around." He drove off in Garvey's car while Travis searched further away from the bunkhouse. It gave Paige a chance to sneak in through a back window.

The phone receiver felt dead in her hand. No dial tone. She put it down then whirled toward the metal cabinet, yanking it open. Grandpa's fireworks collection gleamed inside — rows of black powder cans, coiled fuses, and firecrackers, all arranged with military precision. Her hands moved with desperate efficiency, stuffing everything into a backpack: the explosives, a utility knife, matchbooks and empty metal canisters. She hoisted a rolled sleeping bag across her shoulders, then grabbed water bottles and a roll of duct tape as an afterthought.

A wooden box caught Paige's eye — Adam's old plastic balls, arranged in neat color-coded rows. She snatched a handful, wincing as her palm scraped against a nail jutting from the shelf. Blood beaded along the scratch. Next to the toys sat a mason jar filled with nails and screws. Perfect. She grabbed it, but fumbled one of the toys, which clattered to the floor. She froze, straining to hear any reaction outside. Heart pounding, she crept to the front window and peered out. Travis was heading straight for the bunkhouse. Spinning around, her gaze landed on a sturdy two-by-four leaning against the wall.

A moment later, Travis kicked hard at the door. The sound of his foot smashing into the door echoed in the bunkhouse like a gunshot, followed by a loud thud and an even louder scream as his calf took the brunt of the impact. When he pulled his leg back, large shards of splintered wood impaled his calf. He fell back, screaming. Through the hole in the door and the back window, he saw Paige running away. The two-by-four was still propped under the doorknob.

Bonnet's car skidded to a halt as he spotted Reed and Garvey limping along the road, clothes torn and faces bloodied. He leaned out the window. "Jesus Christ, what the fuck happened to you two?"

Reed and Garvey exchanged a quick glance.

"Nothin'," Reed muttered, yanking open the back door.

"Yeah, nothin'," Garvey added, sliding in beside him.

The engine growled as Bonnet pulled away, eyeing them suspiciously in the rearview mirror.

Meanwhile, Otis was now running scared and confused through the woods. He tripped and fell, badly skinning his knees and hands. He dragged himself back onto his feet just as a pheasant flew out of the brush, causing him to nearly drop dead of a heart attack.

Adam was relieved when Paige finally came back to the cave. She put the sleeping bag and backpack on the ground. "What happened?" he asked.

"Couldn't make it to the main road. Phone's dead in the bunkhouse." She unrolled the sleeping bag. "Help me with your father." They put Eric into the sleeping bag then Paige emptied the backpack. "We need to get ready."

Adam saw all the fireworks supplies. "We could make M-80s. But we don't have..."

Grandpa's eyes went wild as he flung himself forward. "INCOMING!" he hollered, arms covering his head as he braced against a barrage only he could see. Paige and Adam shared a look — part concern, part resignation.

"It's okay, Dad. Everything's okay." Paige then slid over one of the metal canisters to Adam. "Let's start with this."

"That's the way we did it in Bataan," Grandpa muttered.

"Grandpa was in the Battle of Bataan?"

Paige rolled her eyes and shook her head 'no'.

Adam acknowledged with his own eye roll, then took a can of black powder, the roll of fuse line and the duct tape and put it next to the metal canister. "Mom, there's no hole for a fuse."

Paige looked at the canister, thought a moment, then grabbed the utility knife and drove it through the aluminum lid, creating a fuse-size hole.

"Awesome. This is gonna make a big fucking bang."

"Excuse me?"

"The bigger the better!" shouted Grandpa, seemingly part of the conversation, yet clearly not.

"Sorry, Mom."

Paige cut holes in the other canister lids as Adam went on automatic. They continued until they had four bombs. Paige then grabbed the jar of nails and screws. Adam looked at his mother in awe. He watched as she cut a strip of duct tape and placed nails and screws onto the sticky side, then wrapped the strip around the canister. Adam grabbed a canister and did the same.

Eric moaned so Paige checked on him and gave him some water, then she gave some to Grandpa. Grandpa took a sip, allowing the rest to dribble down his chin. "Enough. Save it for the men."

Paige rifled through their makeshift arsenal. "Damn it — — the matches." Adam dug through the scattered supplies beside her. "Try the backpack again." He reached inside, fingers closing around cardboard. When he pulled out the matchbook, Paige snatched it, then froze at the logo printed on its cover. "Radio-Dispatch Taxi," she whispered, eyes widening. "Tom's police radio!"

"You're not going back there?!"

Grandpa tapped his fingers against the ground — S-O-S, S-O-S. "Got to get through to base. HQ, enemy closing in."

Paige loaded up the backpack.

"Mom, I'm really scared. They'll see you."

She strapped the backpack against her chest like body armor and for easy access. "I'm sorry but Grandpa's right." She pivoted away from Adam, shoulders rigid as his trembling fingers fumbled with the buckles. When she faced him again, their eyes met — his wide and glassy, hers narrowed with forced determination. For a moment, neither moved. Then Adam lunged forward, arms wrapping around her waist as she clutched the back of his head, her fingers tangling in his hair.

"You take care of your father and Grandpa."

Adam nodded.

"Good luck, soldier. Make us proud."

"I will, Dad."

CHAPTER EIGHT

THE LAST STAND

The backpack straps cut into her shoulders as Paige pushed through the trees, her breath coming hard. This was it. Her last option. Everything depended upon her getting to that patrol car.

Otis cursed and spat as he rolled down a hill, sending leaves and dirt flying in his wake. "Goddamned stupid hill… Fucking rocks… I hate you, Reed. I fucking hate you." He grunted in pain with each roll and lost his handgun along the way. At the bottom of the hill, he hit a tree with a sickening crack; blood spurted from his forehead and mouth. With the wind knocked out of him, he slowly forced himself to calm down. He started counting backward from one hundred, but the loudness of his own voice only rattled him more. "FUCK!"

Paige hid behind the family cars at the top of the driveway, a long open stretch to the barn — her target. She saw Bonnet's car pull up to the bunkhouse and Travis limp over toward it. The car doors swung open, and out came Bonnet, Reed, and Garvey, the latter two wincing with every step. "What happened?" asked Garvey.

"Nothing," said Travis. "But the bitch was in the bunkhouse."

"More balls than I gave her credit for," said Reed. "Anyone seen Otis?"

"And where's Cindy?" asked Bonnet.

"Gone," said Garvey after a moment's hesitation.

Travis exchanged a glance with Bonnet, their faces hardening. The plan was unraveling, and their promised payday from the bank job seemed to be evaporating with every passing second.

Paige stayed low, crouching between the SUV and the pickup truck, keeping a close eye on the men below. Her attention then moved to the SUV's fuel cap door. She felt a tingle in her stomach and took a deep breath. Paige reached under the back fender and retrieved a magnetic key holder to unlock the car door. She then reached into the backpack, removed the items she needed. Her first action, duct tape the steering wheel into position. Next, Paige rigged the gas tank with a fuse. She lit the fuse, put the SUV in neutral, then moved away and waited — prayed. But the SUV stayed put. She realized her mistake and released the emergency brake. The SUV rolled down the driveway.

Bonnet slid the magazine out of his gun, counted the rounds, then slammed it back in with a satisfying click."When was she here?"

"Just after you left. Couldn't have been more than fifteen minutes ago," Travis said.

"Then the banker and the kid must be hiding somewhere nearby," said Garvey, eyes darting between the trees, his hand twitching toward his own gun.

Reed looked over at Travis, noting the way he favored his right leg, a dark red stain spreading across his jeans — the same leg that had gone through Paige's bunkhouse door. "You can still drive, can't ya?" Travis nodded, jaw clenched against the pain. "Then let's find 'em. And be fucking alert before we all end up like goddamn Travis here."

The menacing SUV roared into view, sending Reed and his crew into a frenzied panic. Their gunshots came rapid and sharp as they scrambled for cover, but Travis couldn't move fast enough — that wrecked leg wouldn't let him. The cacophony of gunfire suddenly stopped as the vehicle pinned

Travis to a tree, ending with the deafening BOOM! With the SUV aflame, Travis burned like a pig on a spit.

Paige made a mad dash to the barn. She entered and looked around cautiously before getting into Murdock's car and trying the radio. It buzzed with loud static. "Hello," she whispered. "I need help. 50 Wanda Drive. Can anybody hear me?"

More static came back at her, then a dispatcher said, "Sheriff's Department. Who is this?"

"Paige Martin. I need…"

"Oh, Paige, how was the party? And why are you…"

"Debbie, they killed Tom." BUZZ. The radio cut out for good.

Paige grabbed at the shotgun locked between the seats and tugged hard, just like Otis before her. The mechanism still wouldn't budge. She bit back a curse then moved on — opening the glove compartment, hoping to find anything useful. Nothing but chewing gum and miscellaneous papers. She pressed the trunk release, her stomach knotting as she stepped out, each footfall heavier with the dread of what she might uncover. When she peered in, there was Murdock's bloodied and crumpled body. Even though she couldn't bear the thought of touching him, she leaned into the trunk and pulled. The sticky wetness of his body and clothing clung to her hands. Her heart was pounding as she heaved his hips to one side, her knees pressing against the car.

She pressed her eyes shut for exactly one second — Tom Murdock, who had knocked on their door to make sure they were okay and gotten killed for it. Paige then rolled his hips, reaching for the holster. It too was empty. Damn. A split second later, she heard yelling.

It was Garvey. "She's gotta be close!"

Now back outside and closer to the bunkhouse, Paige saw the men regroup. She lit and threw a bomb in their direction. It dropped right near the gang, causing them to scramble again to the trees for cover. The BOOM! was a thunderous roar that shook the trees and sent acorns plummeting.

Garvey, Reed and Bonnet slowly peeked out from behind their trees. Then another bomb exploded as Paige ran off. The bomb shuddered the ground as it exploded and debris from the blast rained down around the men, sharp nails and screws cutting through the air as shrapnel. Many got embedded in the tree bark. Garvey's screams were heard over the sound of the men firing blindly in the direction they thought Paige was located. They finally stopped firing and Garvey staggered out. A long screw jutted from his forehead, another from his earlobe. A nail was sticking out of his bicep. He tried to yank out the forehead screw, but only the skin stretched — the screw wouldn't budge. "No, man," said Bonnet, "you're gonna need a screwdriver for that."

Veins bulging at Garvey's temples looked like they might burst. "Fuck, Reed, I didn't come here to get my ass screwed. I'm outta here."

"Fucking A," added Bonnet. They took off running toward their car.

"Afraid of a little firepower?" Reed shouted. "My lamebrain brother woulda handled this shit better than you assholes."

Garvey screamed back at him. "Fuck you, Reed."

"The only one with brains between you two is Otis," screamed Bonnet.

"You pig fuckers." Reed fired like a madman at them.

The men took cover and returned fire. "This is fucking nuts," declared Bonnet.

"I'll keep him busy. You circle around and get behind him," instructed Garvey.

Bonnet took off, then a moment later he heard jingle sounds. He spotted a colorful plastic ball rolling his way. He fired instinctively and blew it to smithereens, then sighed in relief. But something was burning. He turned around and, at his feet, a bomb. BOOM! Again! Bonnet became a pin cushion of nails and screws. He dropped dead with a loud thud as he hit the dirt.

Paige hurriedly dashed in, seized the gun from Bonnet's hand and took off.

Garvey was running desperately towards his car. No way was he going to become Reed's last victim. Reed spotted him get into his car and speed off. He ran off toward it, firing wildly, then stopped and tracked the car in his gun sights and fired once more, hitting Garvey and sending him careening into a tree. A tree limb snapped off and smashed through the windshield, driving the screw deeper into Garvey's forehead. His body went slack, hands dropping from the wheel, and that was the end of Garvey. The only thing that remained was the acrid scent of gunpowder, mixed with the sharp tang of burning rubber, as Garvey's back tires spun uselessly.

Reed then spotted Paige running. She was forced to stop and struggled to catch her breath. Just then, Reed broadsided her and her gun went flying. They clashed in a flurry of fists and kicks on the ground, their movements blurring into one. But Paige was sweating, breathing heavily and clearly at a disadvantage. She then had an opening and was able to give Reed a good kick to the balls that rocked him back, allowing her to grab the last canister from her backpack and fling it unceremoniously at his face. She scrambled back to her feet, retrieved her gun and aimed. But by then, Reed had his gun trained on her too. They froze — standoff. "Nice try, bitch."

Then out of nowhere, Otis staggered onto the scene in a daze, hair matted with leaves and dirt like a Chia Pet, unwittingly positioning himself between Paige and Reed. "It's all your fault," he said to his brother.

"Otis, get out of the way. Move your dumb ass."

Otis stood his ground. "I ain't moving, and you can't make me."

"Don't do this to me."

Otis widened his stance, planting his mud-caked boots firmly in the soil like a scarecrow come to life. His arms hung rigid by his sides, fingers curling into fists inside those black gardening gloves. Sheriff sirens wailed in the distance, their high-pitched screams bouncing between the trees and growing louder with each passing second. Reed's shoulders tensed visibly, his Adam's apple bobbing as he swallowed hard, eyes darting toward the sound like a cornered animal. A soft, almost childlike smile began to stretch across Otis' weathered face, revealing his yellowed teeth and deepening the crow's feet around his bloodshot eyes.

"I ain't going back!" Reed screamed. Before Otis could respond, Reed pulled the trigger, sending a bullet ripping into his brother's chest.

Otis' expression of shock and horror twisted into pain as he stumbled backward and collapsed to his knees. "We could have been long gone," he gasped, as he slumped forward, his lifeless body giving in to gravity.

Paige was frozen in shock. Reed's heart skipped a beat as the sirens screamed closer. His eyes widened with fear. He fired a wild shot at her and missed then bolted into the woods. Her hand shook as she raised the gun and fired back — once, twice. The gun jammed and she frantically fought to clear it. When she finally did, she found Reed again in her sights and fired. He screamed as a bullet tore into his ass just as he reached the safety of the trees. She bellowed, "Now you got another asshole, asshole!" and then stormed toward the sirens until Reed's voice stopped her.

"I know where the family is, bitch. Dead meat!"

Enraged, Paige charged after him. Gulping air, her eyes darted around the woods and suddenly she saw the wounded beast struggling forward. She fired and missed, the bullet hitting a tree just as Reed passed it. He cackled maniacally and fired back, his bullets zipping past Paige before he disappeared, limping into the forest. Paige dropped behind cover, her chest heaving and her hand clenched around her gun.

It took a few moments before she got back into the chase and closed in on Reed. She fired again. The shot kicked up dirt near his feet. He jumped behind a large fallen tree and screamed in pain because of the bullet in his butt.

The sirens came still closer. A helicopter thudded somewhere overhead. Reed tried to ignore them. He positioned himself behind the log and fired off a couple of rounds, grazing Paige in the shoulder. She winced, dropped to the ground, then crawled over to a rock where she checked on her wound. Reed, meanwhile, tore a sleeve off his shirt and stuffed it down the back of his pants in an attempt to control the bleeding.

Paige stayed low, her heart pounding so hard she thought it would burst through her chest, as she glanced up and met Reed's gaze. She instantly raised her gun; her finger pulled back the trigger in a split second. The first shot grazed the top of the log and sent a shower of splinters into Reed's face and neck. He recoiled. Then fired blindly in Paige's direction until his slide locked back. His gun was empty. He crawled away — straight into the path of Grommet, the cat, scurrying past.

Paige got to her feet and quickly scanned the area. Reed was nowhere in sight. She moved toward the log and found blood and a drag trail where Reed had pulled himself away. Suddenly, he popped out from behind a tree, holding the cat up high by the scruff of its neck with his gun to its head. Its paws were up in a 'don't shoot' position.

"How many lives you think this furry fuck really has?"

The cat now saw Paige, wriggled in Reed's grasp and swatted him in the eye.

"Jesus, fuck!"

Reed dropped the cat and it ran straight to Paige. Without lowering her weapon, she scooped the animal into her free arm. Reed squinted through his wildly tearing and bloodied eye, a thin red line trailing down his cheek where the cat's claw had caught him. He leveled his gun at her chest and squeezed the trigger, forgetting it was empty.

Paige's eyes were fierce. Her mind flashed images of the damage Reed had done: Eric bruised and unconscious, Grandpa dropped on top of Reed, the scattered, dead bodies of her friends, Margie's head rolling off. Tears blurred her vision for just that moment.

Still holding the cat, Paige closed the distance between herself and Reed. Her gun was pointed squarely at his forehead, her jaw set and her eyes gone somewhere cold and certain. She stared at him unflinchingly as he closed his eyes, and a smirk began to grow on his lips. But the shot didn't come. As Reed opened his eyes with disbelief, Paige's eyes hardened with a sinister determination. She spat out the words, "Every day is like a week. Every week a year."

Reed's face contorted as spittle flew from his lips. "Go ahead, shoot, go ahead!" His voice cracked with desperation. "You gutless bitch." He swallowed hard, eyes wild. "SHOOT!"

Paige's voice raised over his. "And then another and another," she reminded him.

A police helicopter now hovered overhead. Paige looked up and saw a SWAT sniper aiming at Reed as three other SWAT officers rappelled from the chopper. The pilot looked down and saw Paige turn her back on Reed — and walk away. He picked up his radio to report as the officers handcuffed Reed, who was still screaming, "You fucking bitch."

Back at the Martin house, two white ambulances were lined up in the driveway alongside three Sheriff's cruisers, their red and blue lights painting the twilight. Radio static crackled beneath shouted instructions as the helicopter's rhythmic thrum faded into the distance. Deputies in khaki uniforms swarmed the property like ants as they moved between the main house, the bunkhouse, and the barn, documenting the carnage with cameras that flashed like lightning.

Grandpa, his wrinkled face ashen and lips moving in a silent conversation with ghosts, hunched on the tailgate of the first ambulance while paramedics in blue jumpsuits gently settled Eric's limp body within and hooked him to IVs, his chest rising and falling in shallow breaths beneath a thin blanket. Two other paramedics loaded Deputy Murdoch's body into the second ambulance.

Adam gestured frantically to two stone-faced deputies when he spotted his mother limping toward him, the cat trembling against her chest. He sprinted to her, tears carving clean trails down his dirt-streaked face as they collided in an embrace that nearly knocked them both to the ground before they turned and walked arm in arm toward their wounded family.

Barked commands echoed across the property as Reed, his wrists handcuffed to the metal rails of a gurney, was being hoisted into the same ambulance with Murdoch, his butt wrapped in gauze already soaking through with crimson.

"Wait!" Paige's voice rang out. The paramedics froze mid-lift, and Reed's head jerked up, his eyes narrowing when they locked with Paige's. With deliberate slowness, she lifted the cat's paw between her thumb and forefinger, wiggling it in a slow, mocking wave goodbye — the ghost of a smile curling at the corner of her mouth.

THE END

AUTHORS

Ginger Marin is an actor, author, screenwriter, environmentalist and animal rights advocate. As a former network TV Journalist at NBC News NY, Ginger served as producer and writer for the network's top news shows and various special reports. Ginger is also the author of "Monster on Mars" and "Adventures in Avalon: An Offbeat & Quirky Adult Bedtime Story". To learn more about Ginger's acting and film projects, visit her IMDB page http://www.imdb.me/gingermarin or her personal website https://gingermarin.com. If you want to read how she bemoans the world, check out her blog at http://bioniclady.com

J Bartell, M.A., is an author, screenwriter, and behavior specialist, renowned for developing and teaching his process known as 'Left-Right Brain Suggestibility.' He was previously a licensed Marriage, Family, and Child Counselor in California. In his mid-thirties, J became Chief of Staff at one of the world's largest therapeutic/educational institutes. At that time, he gave lectures and live demonstrations of Pain, Bleeding, and Muscle Control at UCLA and other venues. His clients included people from all walks of life, but it was his worldwide travels on behalf of affluent, private individuals, including heads-of-state, that put him on the radar of the CIA. For more information about J, visit his website at http://jbartell.com

9 798985 512229